FEATHERS

by Steve Piper

An Old Dogs Publishing Paperback

First published in Great Britain in 2023 by Old Dog Publishing
5 Hogshill Lane, Cobham KT11 2AG

1st Amazing Edition 2023
Copyright © 2023 Steve Piper

Printed with love by
www.dcslondon.com

Cover Star: SUSAN NEWMAN
Photo by M Daines of Sunday Mirror 1980

CREDITS

The events and characters depicted in this novel are fictional. Any resemblance or similarity to any actual events or persons is entirely coincidental.

As always, with much love and affection to Melissa and my kids, Charlie and Rebecca, who all share my love for music including Reggae, ska, Two-tone and punk. Thank you for accepting my choosing to be 'anything but ordinary'.

Thank you, Susan Newman, for allowing us to use your stunning image for the cover of this little story.

Thank you, Shirley Marshall for unwittingly providing some of the inspiration for this story though I know your experiences were very different to those of Felicity.

In loving memory of Nicky Porter.

You CAN teach an old dog new tricks

Danny DC   PjH
Mr Bingley   KP   Lilith   Isaac Aquilina
Alan H. Andrea Locking and the Sunbury Skins circa 1980
Gunnislake Mick Waggett.   Garry Bushell.   Lars Frederiksen

PREFACE

Are humans born inherently violent? Or do life experiences create violent humans?

Is it simply a question of 'nature versus nurture'?

What is known is that trauma occurs when people experience and have difficulty coping with an overwhelmingly negative event or series of events. How individuals cope, manage or come to terms with incidences of trauma is as varied as the acts that cause it.

In a thesis carried out in 2006/2007 Daniel J Neller and John Matthew Fabian ask the same question;

'In its attempts to explain horrific acts that humans inflict on one another, the media devote a substantial amount of time to the backgrounds of notorious rapists, murderers, and other violent offenders.

The notion that early traumatic experiences are linked to future acts of violence is appealing on a number of grounds. It is intuitive. It is logical. But the question remains: Is it factual?'

In the study, heading towards some conclusion, they offer;

'The potential effect of traumatic experiences on social interaction appears even more significant than the potential for trauma's emotional and cognitive effects. People with trauma histories are at increased risk for incorrectly perceiving the emotions of others and for misperceiving others' intentions as malevolent.'

Closing the study, it comes as no real surprise that it cannot safely offer any definitive evidence that proves the link between experience of trauma and propensity for future violent acts.

'Although research findings strongly suggest traumatic experiences are related to future perpetration of violence, the precise nature of the relationship remains equivocal.'

'The most reasonable conclusion that can be drawn at this time is that trauma's link to violence is multi-faceted.'

Source: www.crimeandjustice.org.uk

Skinheads are, without debate, the most controversial, most analysed and most revised of youth cults.

The word itself has the power to bond and create or to divide and destroy. Opinions, viewpoints, history and tolerances can be discussed without ever reaching agreement or definition.

Quite simply (as with all youth culture), skinhead is a 'truth thy own'.

One's experience and chosen source of information/inspiration often mesh and this often leads to the individual forming their own inflexible, concrete whole that is resistant to new ideas, newly discovered information and/or difference of opinion.

People choose how they want to carry the moniker forward; they take the bits they like from the fashion, music, attitude, and often, political allegiances and champion that angle.

'Feathers' is a story, a work of fiction. It is a story that includes skinheads depicted in the early 1980s as main characters. It is not a work of history or an academic study of skinheads.

There will no doubt be reflections and descriptions in the narrative where the reader disagrees with the author. This is okay. The author makes no claim to being the all-knowing oracle regarding skinheads.

What the author does have, and holds dear, is a kinship with skinheads that was ignited in the very late 70s through the heydays of the 2-Tone era, when he was a little rude boy, and in to the '80s when he was a skinhead. His experiences and sources of inspiration may well differ from your own.

The question is; 'Does it really matter?'

To many it did, does and will continue to do so.

Feathers, a girl's story, is dedicated to all those girls that dared to make the 'cut'.

I

Jesus!' She hissed from between clenched teeth.

A fan of paperwork scattered like leaves across the office floor. She adjusted her footing with a renewed awareness, her toes fighting for grip through the material of her grey-white socks. The nylon-cotton mix was treacherous upon the slippery surface of the shiny desk top. She had been so engrossed in what she was doing, concentrating intently on the task of opening the window quietly that she had forgotten that she was standing on top of the manager's desk.

She had planned this night for weeks. It would be a shame to mess it up for a moment's carelessness.

She held her breath momentarily, concerned that her exclamation may have been louder than she could afford. She listened intently for any audible threat of hurried footsteps in the lobby, for the angry protest of a thrown-open door. Her lungs let go with relief, the only sound she could hear was the thump of her own heartbeat within her small chest.

She continued with the task all the while aware that time was of an essence. Grasping the cold window handle she pulled inwards to ease the pressure off the catch. She knew from experience that the opening of the old metal-framed windows in the building could be noisy at best and teeth-gratingly cacophonic at worst. She eased the window open. A sharp blast of the late hour snatched at her breath. The night breeze chilled her skin causing goose-bumps to erupt all over her body.

With a last quick glance at the office door, she gripped the frame and pulled herself out through the opening, the soles of her feet finding the cold stone sill. She was thankful to find a heavy cast-iron drain pipe was there, running on down vertically past the first-floor window to meet the graveled path that run alongside the building. She had surveyed the spot whenever they had been allowed to wander the grounds, eyeing up the drainpipe and its offered possibilities but there was always the concern in the back of her mind that she had been looking up at the wrong window. With some satisfaction, she swung herself across and gripped the pipe, her skinny nimble fingers at odds with the cast iron, flaky and rough under her tissue-soft skin.

With careful agility she eased herself down, hand under hand, her socks quickly holed as they snagged and frayed on the abrasive brickwork, her toes appearing through the tears like piglets escaping from beneath a blanket.

She touched down on the pea-graveled path and let out a lungful of relieved breath. It was pitch-black. Her eyes could not adjust no matter how many times she attempted to blink away the blackness. With no torch or natural light, she relied on her instincts and knowledge to navigate her way searching by feel for the verge of lawn that she knew banked the path. She wanted to avoid her footfall being heard and had reasoned that getting on to the soft grass would be a priority if she was to make it off the grounds without alerting anyone.

Her feet found the damp verge as planned. She placed her faith in her senses and headed to where she was sure the front of the house would be. She fought hard not to squeal when she felt the squish of a slug caught between her toes, she stifled a yelp when she felt the familiar sting of a thistle bite in to the ball of her foot. All these were pain and discomfort worth bearing when she finally glimpsed the imposing shadow of the ancient brick wall that skirted the perimeter of the grounds. Tall, rugged and forbidding, it was a formidable structure at least 10 feet in height and as deep across the depth as any wall she had ever seen. Foliage, spiky and dense, crowded the wall's base. It looked impenetrable. This enormous obstacle was split only by the ornate scrollwork of a huge pair of gates. The gates provided the only access to the circular drive that led up to the country building's frontage.

At the corner of the building, she stopped and took a moment to prepare. She knew that it was a hundred and twelve good steps to reach the gates from the position where she now crouched. She had counted them. She was a good sprinter. This particular prowess she had shown on school sports days, being first though the ribbon in the races she had entered and collecting her winner's rosettes with pride. She had enjoyed few rewards so far in her short life but she had enjoyed those small victories. The rosettes pinned to the noticeboard in her dorm room had been left behind.

She waited patiently to pick her moment. Old George the night watchman would be doing his rounds. She knew his routine and his habits. She knew ßthat he was lazy and that he would cut corners. He always did. George was employed to provide night security, to walk the perimeter of the building checking windows and doors but he did no more than he could get away with.

A sudden knife of light flashed from the main door as it was opened sending a slice of brightness across the graveled circle. George stepped out in to illuminated area. He leant against a tall column of stone, one of four pillars that supported the structure that covered the top step. He reached in to the side pocket of his cardigan and pulled out a tobacco tin. She watched as he skillfully rolled himself a cigarette, a man deep in his own thoughts. She saw the flare of a match as he lit the fag. He took a long, satisfied drag then let a plume of smoke out and up in to the cool night air.

He stepped out from the lit porch, down the three wide steps and on to the main circle, his big black boots crunching the gravel. The fag dangled from his lip, his hands tucked in to the pockets of his cable-knit cardigan, his nonchalance clear to see. He ambled to the far opposite corner of the building where he paused.

She knew that was as far as he would go. He rarely ventured further, especially when it was very cold. She also knew that she had about minute before he would perform an about-turn and tread his well-worn path back past the wide steps over to the corner where she waited.

She studied him as he lazily peered down past the long side of the building. Just the usual cursory check for intruders or anything unusual. Satisfied that all was as it should be he rocked back on his heels, plucked his roll-up from his lips and puffed out another long, slow stream of smoke.

She bolted. Her lithe feet whizzing beneath her as she sped towards the gate, her stick-thin arms pumping, her long hair streaming behind her, ignoring the bite of pea-gravel beneath her heels. Stealth was impossible, she had to rely on her speed and agility. She heard George's bark. 'Oi you! Stop!'

It only served to drive her on. At pace, she stared hard at the gates, calculating, identifying the footholds she would need when she arrived at the structure. She made no attempt to slow her approach. She hit the ironmongery hard, grabbing hold, heaving herself in to it, tucking her hands and feet in to its many decorative openings and climbing hard.

She was aware of the agitated scatter of gravel as George's big boots ploughed beneath him. He lumbered towards the gate, puffing and grunting, but knew that she already had the upper hand. She wasted no time looking backwards, confident that she had escaped his reach. She hurled herself over the apex and hit the ground on the other side with such a breath-taking thump her teeth clashed together and her bones rattled. George was at the gate, she heard him wrestling with the hefty padlock and chain. 'Oi! You little cow!

She shook off the impact of the drop and flew off down the black country lane. Her fleet of foot ensuring that she gained enough distance in to the vast darkness of the Essex countryside before George managed to get the heavy gate open. She stole a last sideways glance at the signage that sat atop the stone wall as she fled.

'Great Oaks - Care home for children'

******

The ditch she was sat in stank. Wet and boggy, the ooze seeped through her corduroy trousers, but it provided a momentary haven and importantly, it kept her out of sight of the road.

Felicity had allowed herself a brief stop. A well-earned rest to gather herself. A chance to regain her breath and to try get her bearings. Her adrenalin had spiked and she had been running on it for too long.

Like a fox she was fearful but highly alert, all her senses switched on, watching, listening, smelling for the chasing pack of human hounds that would be out looking for her, noses flaring, seeking her scent. She was uncomfortable, sore and tired but she knew all this was infinitely comparable to being caught and being dragged back to the home.

She knew that it would not be long before some of the 'hounds', would be sent out in cars and the home's minibus to look for her. She had calculated that they could not allocate too many to the task as the other children back at the home in bed would still need looking after. She knew that the manager would have to call the police. That was certain but she felt confident that she could make it out of the area before daylight. Rural police services had better things to do than to go looking for orphaned escapees in the middle of the night.

She checked her hands. They were sore and frayed from the shimmy down the pipe and the clamber up the gate. As she breathed, she felt the bruising starting to come out on her side, the heavy drop had knocked the wind out of her. These issues while causing her some slight discomforts were of no consequence measured alongside her painful, bloodied feet. She had known that going barefoot would be an issue but had no other options.

As always, as part of the bedtime routine all the children were required to place their footwear on racking that was provided before turning in for the night. This racking was placed in full view of the night staff station. She had never had cause to query this procedure until she had made up her mind to perform her own 'Great escape'. Now she knew why they confiscated the girl's footwear. Fetching her shoes had not been a luxury she could afford but the home's rule makers had not accounted for her sheer determination to see her plan through.

It was Steve McQueen, or rather his on-screen character, Virgil Hilts that had provided the inspiration she needed. 'The Great Escape' was a film that proved to be very popular with staff at the home. They had commandeered the TV when it had shown but had allowed Felicity and some of the other children to sit quietly to the rear of the lounge. she had lain awake that night planning her own great escape.

She had admired the characters tenacity and resilience, his application to his mission was admirable. She had developed a crush on Steve and had taken a poster of him from a tv magazine which she hung on the wall next to her bed. It had hung there for around a week before staff took it down, deeming it 'inappropriate' decoration for a girl's dorm.

Despite losing Steve, her hope remained, a small flame that grew stronger by the day deep down in her dark and fearful gut. With patience, diligence and cunning her own plan had slowly pieced together until she felt ready to implement it in full.

She had seen her McQueen poster again, albeit briefly. Glancing through a gap in the staff room door one day she had spotted it pinned to a notice board there.

In the build up to this night she had contemplated hiding a spare set of footwear somewhere on the grounds to aid her plan but was worried that these may have been discovered. She knew that this might have had the effect of heightening security and had practiced caution. She had tried to remain bare foot wherever possible around the building and grounds to toughen the soles of her feet and was often scolded for it.

Regular spot-checks on clothing and belongings were common-place in the home. Some of the staff could be Gestapo-like in their attitudes towards 'caring' for the children. There were good people back there too but they had little influence.

She had liked Mary. Mary was kind but naïve. She liked the girls. She brushed their hair nicely not spitefully. Spoke to them in soft, hushed tones. When Mary was not on shift it seemed to suit some of the other staff. She had heard them say horrible things about Mary.

She felt a pang in her belly as she thought of little George. Her Georgina, her surrogate sister. They had been inseparable in her time at the home. With no brothers or sisters of her own she had quickly adopted George and become her protector.

This loss and any accompanying regret dissipated quickly as she snapped out of her musings. She gave herself a good talking to. George would be so much safer back there now that she was gone. She had sacrificed herself for George's future but it had been worth it. She allowed herself to feel good about it.

Felicity was unsure of how long she had rested but knew that she needed to get out of the area as soon as possible. Her greatest concern was the impending daylight. She did not know how disheveled she appeared but felt filthy, she knew that it would draw attention. Being shoeless was a big problem.

She clambered out of the ditch and to her feet. The rough road cut in to her already wounded feet but she walked on. She knew the road well and the small village that it led to. The issue was that her pursuers knew that too. She needed to get there before the tiny rural population woke and sparked in to life.

She lifted her legs and broke in to a steady trot, blocking out the bite of pain that bolted through the soles of her feet with every step. If there was one thing the home had taught her it was tenacity, an ability to shut down, to take yourself away in your own head.

She thought of London. Huge glorious London. The capital city of England.

Buckingham Palace. Big Ben. The Houses of Parliament. Black cabs. Big red buses. Beefeaters. Bobbies on the beat. Big rivers. Enormous shops like Harrods and Hamleys. Museums that filled roads. Fountains and lions. Flags waving over buildings. Oxford Street. Bond Street. Carnaby Street, Soho and Covent Garden. Bright neon lighting and Piccadilly circus.

Her heel struck a loose stone; the effect was instantaneous. She collapsed to the floor in agony clutching at her foot. The intense pain surged through her. Tears streamed from her eyes as she fought the over-whelming urge to vomit. She was immobilized for several minutes. After some time, her breathing returned to normal though her heel throbbed. She heard the tweet of the dawn chorus, raised her head to the lightening sky and saw the village sign.

******

She kept tucked in where she could, staying tight to the hedgerows and over-hanging trees that threw shade over the road.

Staying tuned in, she listened for the sound of vehicles heading her way. When she thought she heard something she would force her frame in to the foliage pulling branches and clusters of leaves around her, remaining motionless until the danger had passed.

Her bearings had proved good. The road clearly became more maintained and signs sprung up tall out of the verges advising her to 'slow down', clear signs that she was on the approach to the village.

She had no idea of the time but looking to the sky she knew that she had little time before the community broke its slumber.

She hobbled on.

At the edge of the village, she stumbled across allotments. Though the plots were fenced in, the fence was not very high. Knitted with climbing knotweed and bramble she found it easy to scale. Gripping a post, she dropped over and crouched, allowing herself a moment to recce the site. All was quiet.

She scuttled among the muddy rows and vegetable patches, keeping low and remaining alert.

At small sheds and ramshackle storage dotted around the site she stopped to peer through spiderweb-curtained windows.

At a well-plotted row of feathery leaf Felicity stooped and tugged at a clump. The stems came away from the earth easily and she was rewarded for her effort with a cluster of small carrots. The vegetables bright orange was smeared with soil but a very welcome sight to her ravenous eyes. Hurriedly she wiped them against her trousers and drew her hand along the lengths to remove as much dirt as possible.

Satisfied that she had done as much as she could she bit in to the sweet, nourishing flesh. She ate three as she continued around the site.

She came across a structure of bamboo poles and was pleased to find that vines of peas climbed there. She grabbed a few pods, popping them open, chewing the tiny delicacies as she continued exploring the site.

Stopping to investigate another shed she cupped her eyes, scanning the interior through the perspex window. She could make out gardening tools, old plant pots, assorted packaging containing different gardening essentials such as slug pellets and plant food. There was a workbench piled with wads of old newspapers.

Concentrating hard on the back of the door, the timbers peppered with an assortment of nails, screws and hooks haphazardly used for storage, she spotted a heavy black coat.

Felicity tested the security of the window. Suitably reassured, she shoved the pane in as hard as she good and it gave, the plastic snapping in to long shards. As her hand shot through, she was thankful it was plastic and not glass. Clearing the opening of the remaining pieces, she felt sure that she could squeeze through.

Reaching through with both arms, she first she jammed her upper body through, past her armpits. It was no mean feat but she wriggled, squirmed and reached for the floor of the shed for purchase until she was doubled over the window ledge. She swung and kicked her legs until momentum threw her lower body upwards and through in to the shed, dragging plastic pots, a cloud of dusty webs and clusters of drying onions as she went. Lifting herself up, she was pleased to find she had picked up no injuries. She wiped away old spiderwebs riddled with cocooned flies from around her face and neck.

There was nothing useful on the workbench or on the shelves. A quick look around was enough. She could find no use for packets of seeds or a watering can and the papers were all last year's news. The coat was what she had broken and entered for, so she made a beeline for it. Lifting the garment off the makeshift coat hook she was surprised by the weight of it. It was a heavy wool number with a large buttoning closure and winged collar.

Testing the door, it remained secure, padlocked from the outside. She would have to go out the way she had clambered in. After bundling the coat through the window, she took a last look around and was glad she had.

She spied the toes of a pair of boots tucked under the workbench. The leather toecaps had worn thin, steel winked at her through the holes. Pulling them out it was instantly obvious that they were going to be too big for her. Black, ankle-length and sturdy, it was clear they were a man's work boots. She tried one on regardless. As she had feared, they floated on her. No matter how tight she pulled the laces her foot slid up and down freely. Not willing to give up on the boots, she looked around for inspiration and found it.

She grabbed at one of the old newspapers and pulled it apart. Bone-dry paper dust floated in the atmosphere and tickled her throat causing her to hack. She spat on to the wooden floor, her spittle quickly absorbed by the dust there. She scrunched a part of the newspaper up in to a ball then forced it in to the toe of the boot. She did this to both boots until she was satisfied that they would not slip too much. Lacing them both on tight she made haste, clambering back through the entry window.

Back out in the open, she swung the coat over her shoulders and slid her skinny arms down in to the itchy wool arms. She needed to get on. It was important that she got through the village before it woke. She headed back to the road.

*****

The boots were cumbersome and weighed a ton but that was the least of her worries, to Felicity, they were a godsend. After the hours of torture her feet had been through the boots felt like slippers.

She clumped quickly in to the village. Past tiny thatched cottages with pastel-coloured exteriors boasting rose bushes that spilled with bright blooms. Small garages and workshops were dotted here and there, the wooden barn doors heavy with years of crusty paint.

A whirring sound, like a sewing machine, startled her, sending her scuttling in to a sideway. The sound grew in pitch as it approached. A milk float trundled by her hiding spot, the milkman whistling away to himself, busy in his morning's work. He had clearly not spotted her.

In the quiet of the morning, the chink of milk bottles seemed extremely loud. Milky had stopped the wagon to make his deliveries. Peering carefully around into the street she spied where the float had pulled up. She crept out and followed, keeping tight to cover in case the milkman looked back. He continued with his whistled ditty as he carried out his rounds oblivious to the piercing blue eyes that followed his movements.

Felicity waited as he climbed back in and then followed on as he drove the float along to the next group of dwellings. This time she got as close as she dared without alerting him. She waited as he jumped out, whistled around to the back of the float, grabbed a couple of bottles of silver top and swung the gate open to a long flag-stoned path. As quick as he whistled off down the path, Felicity was on the move, she skimmed the float, dipped in to a crate and grabbed a bottle. Laden with her contraband she was away on her heels, all the while conscious that the boots made her loud and clumsy. At the first opportunity she slid between two parked cars crouching there a moment. Looking back, she was relieved to see that whistling milky was none the wiser as to her dip and was going about his business as usual. She waited until he entered another front garden before breaking cover and making her getaway.

Approaching the small village newsagents, she was aware of signs of early morning activity. A boy's racing bike, drop handle bars and gear levers, was leant against the window. Time had become almost indeterminable but she could hazard a guess and guessed that the boy was inside, his bag being packed with the daily rags for his round.

The lone bicycle was a tempting offer. It was a fleeting thought and she discarded the idea quickly. To take the bicycle would cause an immediate furore. The village no doubt experienced little, if any, criminality within its boundaries. The theft of the local newspaper boy's steed would no doubt spark a quick and thorough man-hunt, and that, she could well do without.

Felicity would need to get past the shop front without drawing attention. The village had all the appearance of a tight-knit community. A small well-maintained collection of residences where the villagers probably knew the ins and the outs of each other's toileting habits so she was well aware that a young girl clomping through at dawn, in over-sized boots, cocooned in a great heavy coat, may just draw too much attention.

No, she would continue on foot. It would take longer but she knew where she was headed.

She stooped low and made it past the shop.

At a small village garage with one lonely fuel pump on the forecourt, a man was busy opening for the day's business. The proprietor, slightly stooped, grey haired and clad in work overalls, opened the large doors to the servicing garage with a clatter. A dull yellow light shone out from a tiny kiosk on the forecourt.

Felicity froze in her tracks. A large dog, excited and energetic, pranced around the garage owner's legs threatening to trip him. He shooed it away good-naturedly. The dog was a fully-grown German shepherd. By all appearances, the hound seemed friendly enough but she knew that these canines were valued as guard dogs. The owner wandered into the dark cavern of the service garage. The dog remained on the forecourt. It had given up in its efforts to get its owner to play ball. It paced the area, amusing itself, sniffing the air and stopping for the occasional piss. Felicity cursed her luck.

Suddenly, the dog raised its head searching the air, something had grabbed its attention. An unusual scent, the dog's nostrils flared.

All the while Felicity watched its every move, her anxiety rising. She held her breath for fear of alerting the beast. Her blood ran cold as the dog stiffened its head and homed in on the scent. The canine security made the first tentative steps in her direction.

It may have only been inquisitiveness but she had no idea how the dog would react when it got to her. Would it view her as a friend or foe? She reckoned that it would take issue with her outfit, her smelly old wool coat, grimy torn cords and clumpy steel-toed boots.

The dog got closer and Felicity juggled her choices. It took a micro-second. Decision made she bolted like a stung horse.

She was quick on her feet but she was no match for a German Shepherd in full flight. Her actions had spooked it and it had gone in to full-on seek and destroy mode. She turned her legs as fast as she could move them but the boots were cumbersome and threatened to fly off her flailing feet.

She had almost made it across the frontage when she felt the dog at her heels. Agile and powerful, the animal lunged, clamping its powerful jaws in to the hem of the heavy wool coat. The dogs grip threw her off balance. Felicity stumbled, the vicious tugs of the dog span her, almost sending her to the floor.

The dog wrestled and twisted. The coat was almost torn from her shoulders, she gripped the lapels and tried to wrench the garment from the dog's snarling jaws. As she looked down, terror swamped her. The dog had gone in to kill mode, its eyes wild and wide, froth smeared its jowls. The dog's efforts were all the more terrifying as each tug, snatch and shake was punctuated by a deep guttural rasp.

In a last-ditch effort to free herself, Felicity gritted her teeth and heaved with all her weight. The action sent the stolen bottle of milk spinning out of the big patch pocket, smashing down on to the pavement. The glass shattered, spreading yellow, creamy milk in a large puddle around the melee.

The effect was instantaneous. Initially startled by the noise, the dog released its grip. Within a moment the previously-demonic German shepherd was distracted, forgetting its lethal intent and had zeroed in on the luxurious-smelling spillage. Felicity allowed herself an exhausted breath of relief as the dog lapped furiously at its ill-gotten gains. Felicity needed no further encouragement. She left the dog to its wholesome breakfast and fled.

The owner, alerted by the commotion, appeared from the service bay but he could only scratch his head in confusion at the sight of his faithful friend, tail wagging in satisfaction, its snout soaked white with milk.

Felicity was already gone. Exiting the village, she followed a long, drawn-out bend. Her heart was pounding with effort and elation. The adrenalin spike had yet to dissipate fully and despite the close call she found herself smiling, enjoying the buzz of danger she had experienced. Not long now and she would hit the main road. That was where she would really put distance between herself and the care home.

II

The thoroughfare changed in shape as she approached, widening, like a stream entering a running river. Traffic had increased heading for the dual carriageway ahead and she took extra care to keep a low profile. Box vans, flat-back trucks, whizzed by, some a little too close for comfort, threatening to clout her head with their wing mirrors. The vehicle drivers rarely gave a backward glance, focused on getting to work. As she rounded a yawning bend, she could hear the roll of traffic rumbling along the ancient Roman roadway. She followed the slip road down and on to the main carriageway.

The verge of the carriageway was wide but treacherous, its ground was ragged and undulating. The bank itself was steep making keeping balance a real effort. Felicity was no mountain goat and it hurt her hips trying to make headway along the bank. Huge artic lorries sprayed her with shrapnel; small stones, grit and debris from the inside lane. The noise as they passed was deafening. Occasionally one of the great road dragons would spot her on the bank and sound its great horn in warning making her jump. She grasped at vegetation when she lost her footing, her hands stung from the prickles, nettles and thistles that hid among the tall rough grass.

Relief came at last as she spotted the colourful facade of a service station and café ahead. She hurried on her way but took care. A broken ankle would not help her cause.

Her nose twitched as she approached the café. The aroma of fry-ups beckoned. Sausage, fried egg, bacon, baked beans, fried tomatoes and fried bread hung in the warming morning air. She could almost taste the menu.

Travelers were beckoned in by a long red sign that spanned the front. The large windows were steamed up but she could see that inside, the cafe was already busy with punters hunched over plates of full English, supping brews and smoking cigarettes.

She wandered around the side of the building and in to a vast parking area, all the while thinking about what her next move should be. Lorries of all shapes and sizes were lined up in rows. She could hear the click of cooling engines and smell the heady fug of hot diesel. Heat dissipated from the great grills fixed to the fronts.

Wandering among the wagons she allowed herself to relax a moment. She had been on high alert since leaving the home and was exhausted, both mentally and physically. Her wounds, none life threatening but sore nonetheless, complained. Her feet were rubbed raw, her bones ached from impact and her skin itched with unknown, untold irritations. She was filthy. She rested against one of the many huge wheels of a truck.

'Hello, young lady. What are you up to?'

Felicity froze. The man's enquiry was like the crack of a monk's cane across her shoulders. Resting in her inner world for those few minutes had left her exposed, vulnerable. She woke.

She whipped around to face the man. His arms were crossed above his belly. A belly that threatened to burst the banks of his black t-shirt. She spotted the haulage company logo, woven on his left breast. His Jeans were baggy below his gut, a belt strained in its efforts to keep them up. Virtually bald, he had a smattering of dark hair to the sides and rear. His lips were full and shiny with the grease from his full English.

'Not up to no good, I hope?' He eyed Felicity from top to bottom. Some confusion was evident, no doubt brought about by her choice of fancy dress. He seemed jovial. They stood eyeing each other up for what seemed like an age.

'Nothing.' Felicity weighed up her options. She contemplated making a break for it, forcing her way past the man. An obvious mismatch, a super-heavyweight to her gnat-weight, this would almost certainly lead to more trouble. She did not want any trouble. She had worked too hard to get where ever she was and was not going to risk getting caught now.

She considered trying to slip away beneath the truck. By the time she scrambled through she reckoned fat trucker would be around the other side waiting for her. A tall, fence knotted with bramble closed off any escape route to her rear. Screaming would not help. That would only draw unwanted attention and she would be back at the home in no time and that, was not what she wanted.

'Bit early to be out and about, ain't it, young'un?' The man interrupted her thoughts. He seemed pleasant enough. She sensed no aggression or tension. Despite his size and appearance, he seemed affable. Felicity's brain churned over, trying to find acceptable response. She was relieved when he carried on regardless.

'Not sure it's a great idea for a young lady like you to be out here wandering about on her lonesome.'

Felicity shrugged the shoulders of the heavy coat in reply.

'What's your plans?' The man unfolded his arms and reached in to his pockets. He pulled a bundle of keys and separated them. He looked at her inquisitively.

'I'm going to London.'

He smiled at her and nodded. 'Ain't we all.' He reached up and unlocked the driver's door to the truck cab. 'And how are you going to get to London? It's a fair old way, you know?'

'I was hoping someone could give me a lift.' It sounded naïve but it was all she had at that moment.

The man looked her up and down again. He tilted his head. 'As it happens, I'm London bound. Got some drops to do there.' He pulled the driver's door open. 'You're welcome to tag along if it will help? I'll not charge!' He chuckled making his belly wobble.

Felicity reviewed the situation, then reviewed it again. Her options were not just limited, they were nil. 'That would be great.' She conceded.

The man pulled himself up in to the cab, leaned across and eased the passenger door open inviting her in. 'Hop in then, girl. Make yourself at home.'

Felicity climbed up into the spacious cab. The front screen was wide and tall which, coupled with the height the seating positions offered, gave a great panoramic view out of the front of the vehicle. The man sat quietly a moment and began rolling a cigarette. A silver wedding band glinted as he manipulated a thin paper and tobacco in to a thin straight smoke. He slipped the fag between his lips and with a twist of his wrist he started the trucks big diesel. As the engine throbbed, he lit the fag then leaned across the dash and switched the radio on. 'Name's Bill.' He offered.

'Mandy.' Felicity returned.

Pop music filled the cab.

And when I'm looking in those big blue eyes
I start a'floating round in paradise
You drive me crazy
You drive me crazy

A radio presenter's animated chatter interrupted Shaky's crooning. The man shoved the big gearstick forward and eased the truck through the parking area and out on to the busy carriageway. The wagon trundled on joining the flow of traffic London-bound. As the journey progressed, Felicity relaxed in to the seat. The chugging of the big engine and the rumble of the tyres on the road surface massaged her lower back and legs. The vibration had a hypnotic effect.

It helped to soothe away her aches and pains. Felicity allowed her head to rest against the side window.

A steady stream of radio hits filled the cab space.

One day in your life
You'll remember a place
Someone touching your face
You'll come back and you'll look around

Bill was not much of a conversationist which suited her. Her eyelids became heavy, she allowed her eyes to close.

******

Pressure. Heat and pressure. Unbearable. Claustrophobia.

All movement seemed impossible, her limbs felt paralyzed, she fought to free them but was unsuccessful.

The smell that invaded her nostrils was acrid and disagreeable, it made her gag. It was a smell so real that she was certain she could taste its bitter sting.

She was dreaming, of that much she seemed sure. She tried to control the dream pattern, fought to make sense of the chaos.

Urgency welled up within her as the pressure refused to subside but instead increased and threatened to crush her tiny frame beneath. The heat rose with each second becoming too much to bear. She was terrified, almost suffocating yet something deep in her fought on. A tiny but powerful spark, her own innate instinct for survival.

Confusion fuzzed her mind creating chaotic thoughts and feelings. Felicity fought to make sense of what was happening. Separating the physical and mental discomfort was key. She knew that she had to find some aggression and determination somewhere within if she was to get free.

She sucked in a huge lungful air and held it.

Her eyes sprung open in to a hideous nightmare.

His face was pressed tight against her own. His tongue, slimy and burrowing, was forcing its way between her tight lips. His far superior body mass had her pinned back against the seat making big movements impossible. He found the waistband of her cords, urgent and clumsy, his fingers dug and rooted down-wards, searching for her privacy. She winced as he caught her pubic hair in the invasion.

Heavy pants of sordid desire vented through the man's nostrils. Try as she might, she could not move him off. Weakened by lack of food, lack of sleep and expended energy, she feared the worse.

Unable to open her mouth, a scream lodged in her throat until it faded away. Felicity succumbed to the inevitable.

She relaxed, letting the tension drain away from her body. She allowed her lips, bruising from his insistent attention, to submit.

His hungry tongue slid between as she allowed an opening, writhing and exploring, searching. There in, it slithered and sought her own tongue.

Felicity clamped her jaws down, vice-like. Her incisors cut deep, slicing easily through the spongey, sensitive flesh. The force was deep and devastating. It was designed to be.

Bill leapt backwards; his head smashed against the windscreen. Dazed and panicked, he clutched at his mouth, a viscous cocktail of blood and saliva spilled from between his fingers and clung to his chin.

Felicity spat the bile from her mouth on to his chest then drove her fist in to the blood-marbled face and hands. Bill opened his mouth wide as if to protest. A one-inch piece of tongue dangled by a thread, virtually severed. Her bite had penetrated well leaving the piece connected only by a thin strand of sinew.

She struck again, driving her fist in to the centre of the man's claret moon. This time she used the space created by the assault to make her escape from the cab.

The truck had been parked up in a deserted lay-by, a stop often used, evidenced by the carpet of fag butts, food wrappers, soft drink cans and used condoms strewn across the area. The stench of piss rose up from the gutter. She did a quick recce before scrambling up the bank and pulling herself through a gap in the hedgerow and in to a field beyond.

******

Felicity needed to keep moving. She did not stop until she was sure that she had put plenty of distance between her and the layby. At no point did she look back or ponder on the fate of the driver. That was behind her now, already history. Her only consideration was what happened next and she was going to make sure that she controlled that aspect as much as humanly possible.

It was tough going, the field was deeply rutted, farmland recently ploughed. Small shoots reared their early heads from the neat orderly rows. The vast spread of the field was interrupted by a small copse. Stuck there with no obvious rhyme or reason it seemed a little out of place. It broke the monotony of the scene. A stout oak held the centre, its long limbs outstretched offering shade and cover. Felicity headed there. She needed the rest.

It was not deep or particularly thick but offered respite. The canopy kept the area cool and shadowed. The big oak blocked the morning sun, a carpet of leaves and vegetation covered the ground. The aroma was organic and pleasant and helped to rid her of the smell and the salty, cloying remnants of blood and mucus left lingering after the assault.

A cacophony of leaf and feather erupted above her as a pair of wood pigeons flapped in panic from their perches up in the bows, disturbed by the sudden arrival of a human. She chose a patch of ground and sat leaning against the gnarled, knotted oak trunk. She nestled her shoulders in to its undulations. She lifted clumps of mulch, allowing her fingers to sift the debris. A bright orange centipede emerged and wriggled its escape. She needed to take stock. Her bearings had been skewed by the incident. It had been a close call. She knew she had been lucky to escape and yet she was not panicked.

Felicity was built of stern stuff. She had to be. Tenacity and resilience were attributes she had acquired during her time in the home, very welcome by-products of the insecurity, fear and desperation she had been hit with soon after her arrival there. Felicity boasted an innate strength that allowed her to absorb, adjust and react accordingly to any given situation or incident. This ability to adapt would serve her well. It was something that she was naturally gifted with, something in her core being. She was glad to have it.

A movement caught her eye. Low and stealthy, little movements that disturbed the damp, decaying leaves. There was a sudden eruption as a small mat of leaves leapt an inch in to the air. The cover slipped and exposed a toad. Big eyed and knobbly. Felicity reached out and lifted it in to the palm of her hand. She was surprised to find its skin dry to touch, not at all wet or slimy. The toad sat happily in her cupped hand and squatted there for some time while she looked it over. Her curiosity fulfilled she lowered the toad back among the debris and watched it hop away.

She took this as her cue. Rested and resolved, she got up, brushed leaves from her trousers and headed back out into the field. The copse happened to be sat on a raised area, higher than the surrounding fields. This gave a good vantage point. She could see far and wide. She set her mental compass and followed it.

******

It was not long before she stumbled across a long row of fencing, feather edge paneled, weathered grey. It blocked her progress. Looking down its length, it stretched as far as she could see. She leapt across a damp ditch that ran parallel to the boundary then clambered on to a dense tangle of bramble that covered its bank. Thorns pricked at her shins as she trod the thick shrubbery down beneath her boots. Gripping the top of the thin fencing timbers, she hauled her-self up for a better look. Her arms soon ached making her recce brief. She dropped back down to the bramble. Her first viewing had not offered much. The fence was only part of a boundary that had been created by the building of residential housing adjacent to the farmer's fields. Back gardens extended from the fence towards the properties. The houses she had just viewed were attached to each other so she could see that there was no way through unless she was willing to go through the house itself and that would be a risk too far.

She decided to follow the run of fencing as close as she could. After a few hundred yards she stopped for another reconnaissance. Pulling herself up, she gasped, and dropped back down as quickly. The garden she had peered in to was split by a thin concrete path that ran the length of the garden. A clothes line stretched from a tall pole close to the fence following the line of the path to the rear of the property. What had knocked the wind out of her was the housewife busy pegging the morning's laundry out.

It had been easy to forget that while Felicity was prowling the boundary of the resident's homes, these same residents were going about their daily chores. She recognised she had been too complacent and had got lucky. She had not been spotted by the woman. Satisfied that she had not caused any alarm she went up for another look. She took care this time, treading purposefully and pulling herself up slowly. To either side of the path stretched lawn. Brightly coloured toddler toys and play equipment was scattered here and there. A small child, pre-school age, scooted up the path sat on board a toy tractor, using his feet for momentum and making brum-brum noises. His mum gave a quick glance over her shoulder, checking to see if her ankles were likely to be mowed down. Satisfied that the safety of her lower limbs was assured, she reached down in to a plastic washing basket and pulled another damp item free. She gave it a well- practiced deft flick, straightening the garment before pegging it to the hanging line.

With the woman busy and the toddler scooting, Felicity had a proper look around. Her efforts were rewarded. She zeroed in on the welcome sight of a side entrance that ran down the side of the house. A semi-detached property, a tall wooden gate identified the passageway that separated the building from the neighbouring property. She could not see clearly whether it was secured but felt confident that if needed she would be able to scale it.

She dropped down and shook her arms out encouraging blood to flow back in to her muscles. She would need to pick her moment. Timing would be cru-cial. She would be reliant on her youthful agility and speed. She did wonder if there were others at home. An older child perhaps. A husband enjoying a day off from work. She shook the thoughts from her mind. It made no odds. She needed to get over the fence regardless.

She heard tractor boy end his run up the garden and the awkward scrape of plastic on concrete as he shunted the vehicle around for the return run back towards the house. In her mind she pictured the woman pegging out the previous piece of washing and bending to reach for the next.

Felicity stepped close, gripped the top of the fencing and hauled herself up, her heavy boots banging and scrabbling until she could throw a leg over the top. The woman turned towards the disturbance, startled in to silence by the sudden appearance of the bedraggled youth in her garden. The woman's brow furrowed; confusion etched across her face. Before the woman could scream alarm, Felicity sprung from her crouch. Clear in her aim, she took off on her determined trajectory. Her only focus being to avoid the numerous obstacles that peppered the course and getting to the gate unscathed.

The toddler dragged his toes as brakes to slow his tractor as Felicity sped past, looking up in open-mouthed bewilderment at the alien intruder. A piercing scream filled the air adding urgency to Felicity's dash. The woman spun as Felicity got close to her and instinctively flung the bundle of wet clobber. The garments flew across Felicity's path and slapped tight around her face, adhering to her like suckered tentacles. Her legs kept going, continuing with their rapid rotation while she wrestled with the sodden garments. She was momentarily blind and the wet clothing prevented her sucking in the necessary oxygen for her exertions.

With a cacophonous clatter she slammed in to a large framed item that sent her spilling to the floor. In panic, she clawed at the garments, pulling them free from her head. Then began the fight to untangle herself from the child's play slide. As she pulled her legs clear, she saw the woman bearing down on her menacingly, brandishing the washing line pole like a two-pronged spear. Felicity kicked the slide away from her and spun, making for the gate.

She was relieved to find it unlocked, daring not to look back. She flicked the latch and flung the gate open wasting no time getting through the narrow passageway. The clatter of the improvised spear followed her as the woman flung the pole at Felicity's heels.

But she was away. Away, with no harm done. Out through the side passage, across the front driveway and off down the street of God knows where.

III

The road was sloped and the gradient gave Felicity some relief, she allowed momentum to take over and relaxed a little in to her stride. She zig-zagged through side roads until eventually she met a main thoroughfare. She noticed that her running was drawing unwelcome attention. Had she been suitably attired for morning exercise it would not have turned a head but being that she was dressed like a pygmy navvie and making more noise than a flat-footed rhino there was some interest so she slowed to a walk. She passed a road sign. Shenfield Road. She was none the wiser for the information.

A quick evaluation of her immediate location told her what she needed. The main flow of traffic, pedestrian and vehicular, was mainly heading one way. She hazarded a strong guess that the town centre was in that direction. What she hoped was that the town centre also boasted a train or coach station.

She joined the main drag. Other pedestrians gave her wide berth. She looked and smelt like a tramp. The further along the road she got the more built-up the area became. She passed Brentwood hospital arriving at an intersection, a busy crossroads. Her choices, Ongar Road to her right or straight ahead in to the high street. As she stood pondering which way to go, a woman approached. Felicity had nowhere to go, no way of avoiding contact. The woman was middle-aged, dressed for work, smart and efficient. She held out a hand and Felicity looked quizzically at the small card between her fingers. The woman's finger nails were well painted and clean.

She gestured for Felicity to take the card. 'Come join us, sweetheart. Jesus loves you and you look like you could do with a cuppa.'

Felicity gingerly accepted it. The woman smiled at her sweetly, the lights changed and she crossed the road.

Felicity looked down at the print. Brentwood Baptist church coffee morning.

'Come unto me, all ye that labour and are heavy laden, and I will give you rest.' Matthew 11:28-3

They were words she had seen before. Delicately weaved in needlework. Framed and hung on a wall back at the home. She tossed the card in to the gutter.

Taking the moment as a sign she followed in the woman's wake across the road and in to the high street.

The high street was a shopping heaven for those that liked shopping. Felicity had never experienced that privilege herself, but the pavements were busy which suited Felicity. The crowds offered her some camouflage. Occasionally she stopped, scanning for signs and information that would help get to where she needed to be. Her spirits lifted as she came across the turn off for Kings Road. A well-positioned sign pointed her in the right direction, Brentwood Train station.

The station approach was a hive of activity, she was soon surrounded by the buzz of busy commuters, hurrying and purposeful. The closer she got, the tighter the squeeze. A bottleneck formed as the commuters, heels clicking and briefcases swinging, funneled in to the small suburban train station, a quaint little building of brick with tall arched windows which looked out over to the main road.

Felicity tucked herself in and allowed herself to be absorbed in to the human stream. The pace slowed further as the line filed past the ticket inspector's cubicle. A lone ticket inspector gave token glances at the wafted passes. Felicity had wedged herself between two tall men in lightweight Macintoshes. To her relief she was through unchallenged. On the platform she paused, her cohorts splitting away and leaving her to squint in to the bright sunlight. Felicity searched the platform for information. She was pretty certain that she was on the right platform. The majority of the travellers had remained on the same platform as herself. She looked down the length of platform and spotted a sign that confirmed her instincts. Next train, Liverpool street.

The sensible ones had pottered off to find less crowded spaces where they could wait for the train. Felicity followed suit. She decided to get as far along as she could. She wanted to avoid attention and hoped that the front or rear carriages would be quieter. She had barely settled in position when the distinct rumble of steel on steel caused heads to raise. As the first sign of the chugging diesel locomotive came in to view the activity heightened as folk began manouvering themselves in to position for the embarkment. The chunky, boxy serpent slowed and squealed in protest as the brakes were applied. Many carriages rattled past her before coming to rest.

Heavy doors were flung open with a clatter as the commuters climbed aboard in their droves. Doors slammed noisily behind as the last passengers boarded. Felicity stepped on board and shuffled her way in to the narrow corridor. All seats were taken and passengers were already stood in the aisles.

Some had clearly developed well practiced skills that made their journey less uncomfortable. She watched mesmerized as a city gent, his briefcase tucked between his heels, unfurl a huge newspaper, deftly flicking it and shaping it in some bizarre form of origami until he could hold it with one hand and support himself with the other.

Felicity looked over a smartly dressed lady. The woman's scent was flowery and over-powering, filling the narrow carriage. She was wearing a wolfhound-check suit with all the buttons unfastened. The woman's thin neck was scaffolded in a cream ruff-collared blouse. The collar reminded her of pictures she had seen in history books, of Queen Elizabeth I. It looked uncomfortable. A snug-fitting pencil skirt in the same dog check hugged her stockinged legs. The woman had a satchel hung from her shoulder and in one well-manicured hand dangled a pair of pretty, heeled work shoes. The woman, well experienced in the daily trials of the commuter rush, wore a pair of white sneakers.

The woman seemed to have zoned out. Felicity wondered what she was thinking about. Maybe she was sunning herself on a Caribbean beach somewhere? Or sprawled out on a sunbed by a pool in Spain? Maybe she was anywhere but where she was at that moment, on board the fast train in to the city.

Felicity's legs were throbbing. So much so that it became too much to stand any longer. She slid down and plonked her bum on to the train floor. Wolfhound woman, her daydream broken, looked at Felicity with a grimace. Felicity held the woman's stare for a moment before exercising caution and choosing not to challenge her.

She was sensible enough to recognize that she could not afford to create a ruckus on the train. It was a battle not worth having.

She crossed her arms over her knees and rested her forehead there. The vibration of the train soothed her. Taking a tip from Wolfhound lady she allowed herself to sink in to a doze.

She found herself standing alone at the end of Pall Mall, not a soul was to be seen, not a dicky bird, literally, not a pigeon. She approached a wide set of steps and looked up at the huge monument ahead. The sky was clear, so bright that it forced her to squint. Rubbing her eyes, she looked up at the golden winged symbol; Victory. Victory topped a sky-reaching creation of marble and gilt-bronze that boasted intricate carvings of eagles, mermaids and mermen and hippogriffs. At the centre of the whole monument, sat enthroned, was the figure of Queen Victoria.

Felicity mounted the wide steps and skirted the wide base. Not a breath of wind broke the stillness. Not a leaf fluttered. Not a living thing was to be seen.

Ornately carved pillars topped with an amazing flowering bloom of lighting flanked tall black, wrought iron gates. Large elaborate royal crests decorated the long bars. Felicity gripped the cold iron and squeezed her cheeks between the bars. She gazed in wonderment at the limestone magnificence of Buckingham Palace. Across the vast emptiness of the parade ground, she focused on an arched passageway. Puzzlement creased her face. The passageway was flanked by two sentry boxes. They were both empty. Felicity knew that this was not how it should be. There were no guards. Then she spotted movement. With a yawn, the gate to the passage way eased open. A tiny figure appeared. Felicity's eyes widened in recognition. She had seen the woman many times before.

Who would not recognize the Queen of England?

Resplendent in a flowing white gown slashed from shoulder to hip by a blue sash, her crown sparkling in the sunlight, she floated towards Felicity as if on a cushion of air. Felicity felt as if her face was being sucked through the gate and then she was there. Felicity stared in to the radiance of her majesty.

Queen Elizabeth II reached out and ran her delicate royal fingers across Felicity's cheek. Felicity felt energy course through her spine. She looked deep in to the Queen's eyes and explored the woman's face. A glint flashed from the Queen's face catching Felicity's eye. Felicity spotted the source of the sparkle. A silver safety pin pierced the Queen's septum.

'Hello Felicity, I've been expecting you.'

******

Mild commotion jolted her from her slumber as passengers began readying themselves for the disembark. The train had slowed and was trundling its way in to Liverpool Street station, the last stop on the line. Flanked by cinder brick walls, black with centuries of soot and pocked with the odd daub of graffiti, the train slithered along at a leisurely pace. The same could not be said for the commuters who began jostling and manouvering, preparing for the rush. The train juddered as it finally nosed in to the platform. Doors were flung open before the train had come to a complete standstill, some flash Harrys dropping from the carriage, their legs turning over at pace as they hit the platform.

Felicity was in no hurry. She was much more relaxed now that she had put some distance between herself and her would-be pursuers. Her next test would be to get through the ticket gate without getting collared. For that, she would need the cover of her fellow passengers once again.

Stepping off the train she gravitated to centre of the platform where she tucked herself deep in among the commuters. Some found her too pungent to bear and elbowed an escape. Luckily for Felicity, the crowd being too dense for maneuvering meant that some had no option but to endure her presence. The closer the mass got to the ticket booths the more compact the herd became. She strained to see over the shoulders of those ahead of her trying to gain some idea of the layout. She could just make out the exit gate. It was much wider than the one she had navigated earlier to board the train but to her dismay the gates were heavily manned. She could see at least four ticket inspectors and they seemed to be far more diligent than the previous chap. As she neared, she could hear the good-natured greetings between the inspectors and familiar passengers. One of the attendants was singing.

It was clearly a song he knew well. A song that he was fond of. His performance was unwavering, almost effortless. It was a beautiful voice, organic, from the heart. An instrument of the soul. The man's shiny face beamed with good nature.

Oh, what sweet sensation
Lord, what strange emotion
You got love and devotion
And I won't forget your touch

Though she was hemmed in tight, she felt so exposed. Some desperation set in, her head swiveled, right and left, back and forth. She needed to become invisible.

A noisy, gregarious group of men caught her eye. On their way to the site, they lugged tool bags and metre long spirit levels. Clad in jeans, army surplus garb and heavy boots, crusty and dusty with yesterday's building site grime, the tradesman made their way to the platform exit, swapping banter among themselves, paying no mind to the brush of shoulders and elbows of other passengers. Felicity saw an opportunity for camouflage. She reckoned her big coat and work boots would blend in nicely with the group. If she tucked in tight, she may just get through unnoticed. Decision made, she slid across and weaved her small frame in to their midst. The working boys were a lot taller; she could barely see over their shoulders. Her maneuver seemed to have gone unnoticed. Plaster dust tickled her nostrils forcing her to stifle a sneeze. Felicity tucked her head down tight in to the collar of her coat despite the material scratching her soft ears. The group were brought to a standstill as they arrived at the gate.

'Mornin' lads.'

'Mornin' boss.' They returned.

The workmen's tickets were given the quick once over and they were let through to pop out on to station concourse. Clearing the gate, she let out a long breath of relief and halted, separating from the work crew. She allowed herself an internal dance, a little celebratory moment. She had come along way already. She had overcome all obstacles put in her way and survived this far. She allowed herself to enjoy the victory.

Her victory was cut very short. Her celebration pissed on from quite a height. The strong hand that came down on her shoulder froze her very marrow. She spun in panic to face the singing attendant.

'Ticket please, young man.'

Open-mouthed, Felicity could only look, gawping like a flounder in to the man's deep brown, shiny face. A wiry moustache framed his top lip and his hair was clipped short, a razor parting split his tightly curled hair to the crown. It was a gentle, calm, friendly face.

Instinctively, she tried to shrug his hand off but it was ineffective. The man's grip was too firm and easily held her petite shoulder. And yet, there was no hint of aggression or spite in his action. It was as if he was almost relaxed.

It was a warm morning but he still chose to wear his dark uniform jacket over a pale blue work shirt. On the jacket lapel a British Rail badge with a red and silver motif was pinned.

And there was another warmth, emanating from the man himself. Even as he spoke, doing his job, carrying out his role, making his enquiries, it was clear that he meant no harm. His appearance though belied his strength, his capability. He was not a walk over. 'Have yuh a fare or not, young man?'

Felicity frowned at the repeated inference regarding her gender.

'I must see yuh ticket for the travel.'

Felicity considered going in to attack mode. It was her fail safe option and had proved successful so far. But something prevented her being able to draw up the necessary venom for any attack. Yes, there were people everywhere, too many eyes and ears, that fact in itself made it risky. But that alone would not have prevented her from doing what she felt was necessary to carry out an escape. No, there was something else, something deeper that subdued her attack dog instinct. It was the man's aura.

His demeanour had the ability to neutralize any aggression she may have been able to muster up. She could genuinely find no incentive or desperation worth hurting the man for. His inherent nature, pleasant, gentle, calm, poured milk on any disturbance in her gut; soothing, cooling and calming; dousing any violence she would otherwise have relied on to get herself out of this predicament.

Felicity slumped, emotion forming in her throat. She would not cry even though she wanted to. She felt his fingers ease their grip on her shoulder. 'Yuh have no ticket, have yuh.' It was a statement, not a question. He lowered his head to look at her face. It was then that he realized his mistake. He gave a little chuckle. 'Well then! Where you headed, young lady?' He emphasized the 'young lady' drawing it out, almost in offer of apology.

Felicity noticed his accent was very strong and a relaxed cadence to his speech awarded a musical quality. He clipped sentences, missed out words.

'Where you from?' Felicity countered. The man's face widened with surprise at her cheeky response.

He chuckled. 'Well now child, I man from the islands, Jamaica. You know where Jamaica is?'

'Of course, I do, I'm not stupid!' Felicity was well versed in geography. She soaked information and facts up like a sponge. Reading was one of her loves. It was life experience she lacked not learning.

'I can see dat, girl. Definitely not stupid, dat is clear to me. Yuh got dis far innit!' The man's mannerisms were mildly animated, he raised his eyebrows comically and shook his head slowly side to side. 'So, you is definitely not stupid!' he chuckled again. 'Yuh get me?'

He did not wait for her to answer. 'So, now you know where I'm from.' He dropped his hand, lowering his face to hers. 'How 'bout you enlighten me a little as to what you're doing, riding me train without fare.'

Felicity lowered her eyes. She had an overwhelming urgency to blurt everything out to the man. It would be a huge off-load but it was a burden she knew that she, herself, would have to carry alone, at least for a while longer. 'I'm trying to get home.' It was untrue but caused no harm, Felicity reconciled herself with this simple justification.

'Home is where?'

Felicity searched her brain. She conjured up a mental image of the Monopoly board game. She parted the two leaves of the playing board and ran her little pewter boot around the board's colourful perimeter. She stopped at the light blues.

'Islington, the Angel.' She grimaced slightly, instantly aware that it sounded daft. Who did she think she was kidding?

The man nodded in recognition. 'Chapel market! Nice place, some posh yard there!' His face then turned back, business-like. 'Well, miss, before you forward to the Angel of Islington we need to settle up.' He sighed. 'How you intend to pay yuh fare?'

'I can't.' It was all she had. No point in making up some other pathetic excuse.

The man breathed in heavily. He smoothed his moustache with his thumb and index finger. He took in the bedraggled state of the young girl before him. He wrinkled his nose at the soiled, smelly coat and the too-big boots. His chestnut-brown eyes felt the sear of her deep sapphire-blue eyes. It was all a confused, sorry mess, that much he could tell.

He was a diligent employee, always had been. He carried his duties out to the best of his ability, always positive in approach and aiming to please. That was why he sung. He sung because he was happy, he loved his job. Yet had he not needed a lucky break on occasion?

Arriving in England in 1960, the world had been a very different and, not altogether pleasant, place. He had relied on his wits and the generosity of strangers to navigate those early days. Finding a job had been relatively easy, finding residence was altogether more difficult. Folk was very wary of the new immigrants and, at worst, hostile in attitude and behaviour towards them. He had used his head and settled in an area where early immigrants before him had already made their home and were already becoming a respected part of the community.

Now look at him; 20 years in England, full employment on the Railways, well settled with a wife and two children, a home of their own, a nice car. He had done well.

He reached his strong hand into his big jacket pocket. He pulled out two silver coins, each one worth two shillings if you were pre-decimalisation or ten pence if you were born after 1971. Without word, he reached over and slipped them both in to one of the big patch pockets of Felicity's coat. He patted her shoulder turned her with ease, giving her a bump start with aid of a small shove in the small of her back.

'Bless you child. Run along nuh, before we change me mind!'

Felicity was taken aback by the man's gesture. She was sure her number had been up and had not expected any leniency let alone this much kindness. She stopped awkwardly to look back at the man.

She met his eyes and smiled. 'Thank you!'

He made a 'get along' gesture with his hand. 'G'wan, don' let me catch you riding without fare again, you hear?'

'I hear yuh.' She chirped and was gone.

Winfred watched as the little sparrow weaved her way through the crowds until he could see her no more. He took a deep breath and sang out.

Now there's nothing left for me to say, girl
Than stay in your world
You got someone's soul deep inside, girl
And love that's richer than gold
Oh, what sweet sensation

IV

What a kaleidoscope of imagery and colour the station was. Felicity found it difficult to walk straight without being distracted by something, looking up and around, her neck ached from the effort. Its vastness seemed incredible. A sonic soup of a thousand different sounds swarmed her. Porters shoved tall wheeled trolleys, the cages stuffed full with packages and mail, around the concourse. City workers sped to their work, heels clipping and scuffing as they went. Workers, travelers and tourists meandered among this seemingly chaotic scene. Gorgeous smells of cooked food seemed to be deliberately wafted from booths and stalls mingling among the station users, teasing and tempting them.

Felicity's nose wrinkled as a waft of fresh baking passed under her nostrils. She fondled the coins in her pocket rolling them between her fingers as she gawped at the display of edible jewels laid out behind the glass. Shiny iced fingers glowed alongside coconut-haired London cheesecakes. Heavy bricks of bread pudding flexed next to cherry-nippled Chelsea buns.

Her mind made up she joined the customers inside. Waiting her turn to be served she was oblivious to the other customers distaste, her only focus on getting her prize. She traded the silver coins for a Chelsea bun and a few coppers change. Felicity tugged it from the paper bag and gasped audibly at its size. The bun was lavishly iced and sticky. Its shiny glace cherry a lone gem on a rink of white icing. There was no time to appreciate its splendor, to savour its beauty. Intense hunger put paid to any artistic critique as she jammed a great wedge of the pastry in to her mouth. A burst of pleasure filled her as the sweetness stimulated her glands and soaked her senses. The bun had not a chance of survival, she almost choked herself as she wolfed the remainder of the pastry down.

Satiated for the time being, she looked for an exit. It would be another roll of the dice; she had no idea of where exactly she was headed. Luck would have to play a big part.

A particular exit looked popular. She followed the commuters and travelers making their way out of the station. All good manners and decorum seemed to have evaporated. People rushed and jinked in their hurry to get to where they wanted to be. A short bustle found Felicity exiting in to bright daylight.

She stopped for a moment to gather her bearings. Behind her the station entrance, a brick-built central apexed construction hemmed in at both ends by two pillars topped by stubby lead-worked steeples, spewed its human bile in to the street. A clock face was fixed up high on one of the pillars. Felicity checked; it was 9:15 am.

As she ventured on to the main drag, she became disorientated once more. A sign assured her that she was stood at Bishopsgate but which way along the road's length she should travel, she was unsure. After a few minutes of indecision, she plucked up the courage to stop a young city boy as he hurried along. Her assumption had been that he looked at home, familiar in his surroundings, like he knew his way around the area.

'Excuse me.' Mild agitation furrowed his brow. Her approach was clearly an annoyance, an inconvenience.

'Sorry, mate, I've got no cash on me.' It seemed a well-practised response, almost instinctual. One that he had used regularly. He tried to skirt around her but she was insistent.

'No, no, wait.' Felicity held his forearm. He looked down at her hand then back at her face, his initial mildly agitated frown morphing in to a look of mild concern. His responses, whether agitation or of concern, lacked conviction. His mind was clearly on other things.

'I just need some directions.' She racked her brain to think of a location, a London landmark that was familiar to her. 'I need to get to Oxford Circus.' It was an odd choice. One that popped in to her head out of the blue.

The man gave a little harrumph. 'Blimey! You've a little way to go, mate. Why didn't you get on the underground? Would have been there in a jiffy.' He gestured to a bus stop. 'Best off grabbing a bus over there. Goes straight through to Great Titchfield street. That's right close to Oxford Circus. Takes about 15, 20 minutes.'

Felicity felt the weight of the bun in her stomach. Her bus fare was being digested while they chatted.

'Anyway,' City boy pointed her down the road. 'It's that away.'

With some resignation Felicity committed herself to another hike. At least she had some idea of where she was headed. Oxford Circus! That bloody Monopoly board had a lot to answer for. At least now she had a bellyful of pastry and sugar to work off.

She followed 'Ye Olde Bishopsgate' until it crossed with London wall shooting off to her right. It seemed an obvious choice so she took it; follow the wall.

That old London wall was a remnant of Roman occupation. An old defensive line, the old boundary of early London, it was now a busy thoroughfare. Commercial buildings, tall and imposing on both sides of the road, seemed to deny its history but it was there. Between the gaps in the buildings, ragged, stone structures, remains of that roman and medieval past peeked through.

Felicity gritted her teeth. Though she did wonder how long the road could really be, she kept going. She had no other option. Eventually she arrived at a large roundabout and allowed herself a breather. The big rotary was only a pause but a welcome one. She leant on a roadside barrier. Vehicles whizzed around the great circulatory, tooting horns and revving engines, it was dizzying. She read a large signpost directing tourists and sightseers to the Museum of London. She wished that she had the time to pay a visit. There were so many things that she wanted to see and do in her life. In her mind, learning, knowledge and education was a gift and she loved to learn new things. She had always grasped any opportunity for knowledge despite any obstacles that appeared, and she boasted a hungry curiosity as well as a capacity for mental storage that was to be envied. As well as having an academic mind, Felicity was blessed with a fearlessness when it came to trying new things. She was very much a 'nothing ventured, nothing gained' kind of girl. Unfortunately, the museum would have to wait. She needed to press on.

Taking the left turn off the roundabout she headed down Aldersgate Street following its hard right at the bottom in to Newgate Street. She was really feeling the pace now. Her legs had eaten up the miles. Her calves ached and her hamstrings twanged yet she was able to keep moving. She had developed an odd ability to separate her mind from the discomfort in her feet. Her pain threshold had risen to a degree where the pain she had previously been averse to had now become the new normal.

She kept her focus on the road, it seemed never-ending. It stretched on forever as far as she could see. Newgate was a name familiar to her as she passed the junction with the Old Bailey. She remembered that it was the area where the famous Newgate Prison once stood. It led in to historic Holborn.

The tangle of highway in front of her almost broke her. There seemed to be no clear way ahead to her, no obvious through-route, just a chaotic intersection of roads through that part of the city. Any earlier fire of wonderment in her travels was doused. The over-whelming sight of Holborn junction had caused her a momentary loss of composure. That earlier child-like curiosity had now been lost to the necessity to focus her energy on staying upright and moving forward. She fought to keep her head up and shoulders back, the effort so much that she would occasionally groan out loud startling passers-by. They gave her weird looks, to them she looked just like another mad London tramp.

She began to lose sense of place and time, feeling as if in a bizarre hallucination. A horn honking or a sudden shout sparked her dwindling supply of adrenaline, rousing her from her standing slumber but she quickly slumped back in to her upright daze. Holborn was threatening to be her nemesis.

She passed a passageway. Glimpsing through it she saw a flash of greenery among all the greys. Felicity pulled herself away from the main road, slipping down the narrow side alley. It came out in to a residential square. Tall Victorian-built houses surrounded a central residential garden, a lush well planted area bordered by low iron railings fat with yearly applications of green paint. Felicity let herself through a squeaky gate and followed the oval path. It was as if she had stepped into a sanctuary, a parallel existence to that which she had been experiencing only moments before.

It was a lovingly cared-for square. Trees were well placed creating shade and the low borders were bright with a wide variety of blooms. Felicity allowed herself to enjoy the cool air on her face and the different scents that replaced the fug of traffic fumes. She stopped at a bench and sat, taking the weight off her aching legs and feet. Feeling relaxed she slid around, bringing her legs up and on to the slatted seat. She laid back against the wooden armrest, Tucking her hands behind her head. She looked up in to the gently swaying canopy above, watching the breeze waft through the leaves of the tree. Slashes of sunlight broke through the tree branches as they moved. She closed her eyes, focusing on allowing her muscles to soften, sinking into a slumber.

'Get the fuck off my bench!'

Felicity's eyes popped wide open, startled, and stared, horrified, into something almost indescribable. It was a wretched, wreck of a face that stared back at her, deranged and threatening. The eyes seemed hollow and pinched, tiny apertures in a mound of flesh flushed with blood, the pupils just pinholes. The nose was pudgy, veined and orange-peel textured. The lips were swollen and flecked with spittle. A scrubby, stained beard trembled with agitation. Ingrained dirt highlighted the man's life lines. He was bent over her, so close that she could not sit up without bashing heads.

'I said, get the fuck off my bench.' The voice was rasping, it came deep from his throat. His breath was hot on her cheek, hot with the fuel of alcohol and the stench of rotting gums. The man's hair was a matted, unwashed bird's nest of grey and ginger. Tendrils dangled from his forehead across Felicity's top lip, clawing and scratching. She tried to twist head away. She shrugged down into the bench trying to create more space between them. A fist clubbed downwards thudding on to her chest. The blow hit her hard in her solar plexus knocking the wind out of her. Despite her predicament, she had not expected the assault. She was completely defenceless.

Doubled up on the bench, she wheezed frantically as she fought to suck in air. It was all she could do to maintain some focus as she fought to recover. The man was clearly unwell and beyond reason. Her gender was clearly no defence, as irrelevant to him as most other things in his life.

'I told you before!' His rant continued. 'Don't go on my bench. Its mine!' Strings of sticky mucus spun from his mouth and caught in his beard. 'Mine!' He repeated. 'Mine, you bastard!'

He swung again. It was a wild, animal-like movement but one full of intent. She moved her head quickly. And it saved her. This time he missed his target, his knuckles striking the gnarled wood of the bench behind her head. He yelped in pain and the bottle of red wine he was holding with his free hand fell to the floor, claret spilling from the neck forming a puddle around his ragged footwear. This set him off, the loss of his medicine too much to bear. He let out a roar of anguish as he stooped to save the contents glugging away in to the lawn. She seized the moment and spun off the bench.

Having rescued his prize, the man took a slug and set off after her across the park; a great, scruffy, hairy yeti, arms held aloft, wine bottle clutched, all the while, screaming obscenities and threatening harm. She was terrified, the man's commitment as he chased her through the carefully planted flower beds sent flower heads and petals out in an explosion of colour. She wasted no time opening the gate. She flung herself, one-handed, over the garden's low-fenced boundary and hit the other side running, straight back through the passage from where she had come. She could hear the man's tortured yells ringing off the high walls as she sprinted out on to the main drag once again.

V

It was with some relief that her Holborn nightmare came to close. Arriving at St Giles on the heath, it was here that Felicity dithered, a road swung up to the right or she could go slight left.

She decided to go slight left.

The whole architecture and atmosphere, the character, of the streets changed again. It was an area that promoted consumerism, shopping and entertainment. She came across a busy T-junction, a road sign high on a building told her that she was at Charing Cross Road.

This time she went right.

All change again. Books and bookshops. Felicity was fascinated. She loved to read and could not help but pause to peer through the many store windows that catered for those of bookish persuasion. It was a welcome distraction from her aches and pains. Antiquarian, special interest, military, the arts, spiritual. She wished she had time to browse the shelves inside but had other priorities at that moment. Anyway, it was doubtful she would be allowed across the threshold in her current garb. She dreaded to think how awful she must smell. She thought it odd that one could not smell one's own stink. By now, she had got used to the odd stares and looks of concern. She was aware that she looked like a runaway vagrant and though these looks of distaste and inconvenience made her feel self-conscious she was more disturbed by the anonymity that most pedestrians awarded her. It was the nonchalance that most displayed that showed how normal it had become to see homeless youths wandering the streets of London.

All human life flowed around her like a stream, Felicity was there, just a minor inconvenience, a pebble, causing a minor ripple, as she wandered among them. The jarring barge of an unintentional shoulder or the clip of an elbow in her midriff or the bump of a briefcase against her thigh reminded her of her position. No apologies were offered. That would have taken up their time.

Hunger chewed at her insides. The energy from the sticky Chelsea bun was long-a-go spent. Her stomach twisted and groaned, she felt almost delirious, desperate for sustenance. It got to the point she could think of nothing else. Any hint of food in the air made her nostrils flare. Her nose twitched as she caught the sweet scent of fried food. Her senses had been sharpened by hunger. She turned instinctively to the source of the smell. She followed her nose, sliding and slipping among the human stream ahead of her until she found herself standing in front of a fast-food outlet. She looked on in wonderment at the buildings vast glazed frontage, its bright red and yellow livery, neon-lit high overhead, a vision so gaudy and bright to her that it made her squint. In all her meagre years she had never had the opportunity to visit such an establishment. She had had fish and chips on the very rare day trips that the home had organized to the local seaside resort but had seen nothing like the establishment that she was stood in front of. Saliva flooded into her mouth as she watched patrons cramming fat burgers spilling glutinous sauces, into their mouths. Plucking clutches of French fries from bright cardboard cartons cramming them between greasy lips. She swallowed hard as she watched them suck at thick straws, drawing up sweet root beer and fizzy coca cola, watching them strain, threatening to cave their cheekbones in, as they pulled at thick milkshakes until their eyes crossed with effort. She turned her attention to a couple who had just been served. She watched their movements intently. They chatted as they searched for a free table. She eyed them enviously, their tray piled with burgers wrapped in greaseproof paper, fries spilling out of the cartons among tall paper cups filled with cold Coca-cola. They found themselves a spot close to the front window, smiling and chatting away to each other, completely engaged in each other's company. All the while, oblivious to the pair of desperate young eyes staring at them through the huge window.

Felicity had made her calculations. Speed and accuracy were paramount if she was to be successful in the execution of her plan. She timed her movements perfectly, slipping past a customer that was exiting the premises, she darted in through the opening, once inside she swiveled on her heel, did a sharp right and quickly approached the couple's table. She flung out an arm and plucked the burger from the girl's hand as she was about to take a bite leaving the young woman empty handed. The girl gawped at her beau, her mouth opening and closing like a thick-lipped carp left flapping on a riverbank. Felicity was already gone, back out on to the street and away with her take away.

******

The burger was like manna from heaven. The fact that it was stolen failed to taint any of her enjoyment. She chewed each mouthful for what seemed like an age, savoring each morsel allowing the plethora of different tastes and textures to soak her taste buds. She was unsure about the pungent green slivers of vegetable matter that were tucked in among the good stuff but ate them anyway unsure where or when she may get her next meal from. Beggars could not be choosers.

The alley she had stumbled across was narrow with walls that reached high. With dark-red-brown mottled brickwork streaked yellow in places, it was clearly part of old London. She had entered the alleyway with caution and was relieved to have found it to be empty, just piles of cardboard boxes and rubbish bags stored at the back doors of local businesses. She had grabbed a couple of the flattened boxes used them to sit on, her back leaning against the wall. She enjoyed the solitariness of the moment. Like the gardens earlier, the alley offered the uncanny characteristic of dampening any street noise, the hustle and bustle, even though she was aware that just metres away from where she sat, at the alleyways entrance, all human life and endeavour continued. Reluctantly and not without some regret, she finished the burger, she screwed the wrapper into a tight ball and clutched it in the palm of her hand. She leaned her head back against the rough brickwork and closed her eyes. Her thoughts darted through her mind like a thousand agitated wasps, her eyelids flickering with disturbance. Gradually tiredness dampened the buzz of her over-active mind. It had been one hell of a long day. She had no idea of time but knew that dusk was falling. She focused on the rise and fall of her full belly as she breathed. She savoured the remaining remnants of the burger, pungent in her mouth until the last. Her lids grew heavier, she was so tired, she succumbed without a fight.

VI

When she woke, she was disorientated. Her bum was numb from sleeping in a sitting position despite the cardboard she had laid there. Completely exhausted, she had slept through the night. She blinked hard, scattering the residue of sleep from her lids.

She opened them fully and looked straight across at a boy sat directly opposite her; his body positioned in a mirror image of her own. This sleeping lark was treacherous. It seemed she could not risk even a brief moment of shut eye without waking in to another incident. For the third time in less than two days she had been caught napping and now had to dig herself out of another shitty hole. First the pervy lorry driver, then the insane bench tramp, and now, rat boy.

Ratboy was young, that much she could tell. He certainly had no need for a razor yet, not a patch of fluff graced his chin. His head was shorn to a number one fuzz, his ears stuck out, his top teeth protruded, like a rat's. He offered her a grin; a black gap separated his two front rodent teeth. The smile did not match his eyes. His eyes were dulled, flat, almost devoid of life.

'Alright mate?' It was as if he did this sort of thing every day of his life; snuck down alleyways and ogled young girls catching some beauty sleep. Felicity did not know how to respond. She was unsure what was required of her so she chose not to. Defensively, she clamped her arms tightly around her knees.

'I'm Terry.' He was not put off easily. Ratboy, otherwise known as Terry, was clearly a local, a Londoner. His accent was enough to clarify that much. 'What you doing around here on your own?' His manner was very relaxed, convivial. Despite her resolution not to interact, Felicity shrugged.

Terry wriggled and ferreted around in his jeans pocket eventually pulling free a packet of cigarettes. The packet had somehow survived the ordeal of being wedged in his tight jeans. And his jeans were tight, tight enough for Felicity to notice the bulge in the denim of the boy's meat and two veg cocooned there. He teased a stick out and flicked it up between his lips. He extended the packet in her direction offering her a fag. She shook her head a little too quickly. She wondered if it appeared rude. She didn't want to antagonize him.

Not yet anyway. She needed to suss him out a bit. She studied him as he clicked a lighter to flame and lit the fag. He took a drag and puffed out a cloud.

'You don't look like you've been here long.' He nodded at her. 'Look like you could do with a good bath though!' He chuckled. Felicity fidgeted in the thick coat and heavy boots. 'Looks like you've had a bit to eat though,' Terry pointed at her chin. 'You're still wearing some of it!'

Felicity dragged her coat sleeve self-consciously across her chin removing the dried crust of burger relish. Terry blew smoke rings out to the side. There was no hint of aggression or intent on his part. That much she could tell but she kept her guard up, determined not to get herself in to another predicament. Felicity kept her gaze locked on him, she was alert and ready. Her trust had been well tested and she had learned to offer little of herself. She gave a sideways glance down the alley towards the main road checking her escape route was clear. Terry was not a big rodent, she felt reasonably confident she could be a handful for him. She tried to guess the boy's age but found it an impossible task. His features although youthful seemed aged, with more depth than she thought should have been there. She could not exactly say what it was that gave her this impression just that his eyes did not fit.

Terry broke the silence. 'Funny old place London. It's like a magnet ain't it?' He observed. 'Where else can you run to where you can disappear as easily and quickly as you can in London? It's no wonder is it that us lot make our way here?' He left her a pause to reply. She chose not to comment. 'I've lived in London all my life. Not here but in South London, to be exact. I had to get away. Me mum met a new bloke.' He paused again and shrugged. 'He didn't like me and I fuckin' hated him!' He chuckled. 'Man, we had some rows! He was a fuckin' bully, thought he could give me a hard time. Not me though.' He pointed to a feint scar under his right eye. 'He did this, a little reminder of the time he threw a glass ashtray at me because I told him he was a waste of space wanker!'

'What did your mum do?' She mentally kicked herself, her resolve had broken, curiosity had won.

If Ratboy noticed her regret, he never let it show. 'Fuck all. She just took his side as usual. Told me that I was an awkward fucker who just wanted to make things difficult for her!' He shook his head lightly. 'I gave up in the end. Packed me bags and headed up west.' He stretched his legs out, crossing them at the ankles. 'It's where we all end up, ain't it!'

'Is that where we are? Up west?' She asked.

Terry looked at her quizzically. "Well, yeah, that's what we tend to call it.

The west end.'

'Of London?' She quizzed.

'Yeah of course.' He looked at her as if she was simple. 'Why are you here?'

Felicity shrugged. 'Same sort of story as you I suppose. Better here than there.'

She was warming to the rodent. Terry seemed a half decent bloke.

'Well, you can do alright here if you choose your friends and acquaintances carefully.' He flicked the fag butt down the alley, sparks bouncing off the concrete. He rose to his feet dusting the backside of his jeans down with his hands. He held his hand out for Felicity. 'C'mon, I'll show you my pad.' She took his hand and allowed him to haul her up. He chuckled at her big black boots. 'Nice pair of daisies by the way!'

'Daisies?' Felicity queried.

'Daisy roots, boots! Blimey! You are green ain't you!' Terry tugged her through the alley back out on to the busy thoroughfare once more.

******

Terry walked quickly, guiding them deftly, weaving through the hoard of pedestrians until he swung off in to a side road. He pulled her in to a doorway. The paneled door was grey and crusty with years of road grime. Index cards pinned to the door frame offered 'models'; Brunette, blonde, red, alongside French, corrective and specialism. He ushered her through and in to the hallway.

Her senses were assaulted. She tried not to bring her hands to her face concerned that she may cause offense. It was not a dirty smell but one of attempted sterility. It was the smother of industrial-strength disinfectant. Terry led the way in to a reception room.

'Hello Terry. Who is this you've brought with you?' The woman's shrill voice was as disagreeable as the overpowering odour that permeated the place. She stared at Felicity making her fidget awkwardly.

'This is Felicity. We just met. She's new to London.' Terry announced his new found friend.

The woman continued to stare hard at Felicity. She wrinkled her nose. Felicity had forgotten how grubby she must have looked.

Terry tilted his head. 'She needs a bath, Audrey. I said that she could get cleaned up here.'

'You should check first Terry You know that. I don't like surprises.' Audrey puffed out a long stream of cigarette smoke. 'How old are you, Felicity?'

'Sixteen.' Felicity fidgeted again, feeling heavily scrutinized. 'It's no bother, miss, really. Terry shouldn't have asked.'

Audrey allowed herself a cackle. 'Miss? I've not been a Miss for a very long time!'

The woman's hair was voluminous, wispy and curly, like candy floss. She wore earrings that were gaudy and chunky, dangling heavy, threatening to pulled her lobes free from her ears. Felicity wondered that the woman's hair was not caught alight by her cigarette it seemed that flammable. Audrey wore a lot of make-up too; her lips were sticky with thick red.

Felicity let her eyes wander away from the woman. She scanned the lounge. The space lacked something. Swirling in gaudy Axminster carpet, a tiled fireplace created a focal point, with an alcove to either side. There was nothing homely or cozy about the room. It all seemed very deliberate. Business-like. There was seating and plenty of it. Armchairs and two-seater sofas aplenty were plotted around the room separated by small coffee tables. Heavy, blocky marble ashtrays and matching marble cigarette lighters and small piles of men's lifestyle magazines spread across the table tops. The tall walls were decorated in a heavy flock paper split by a painted dado rail and interrupted with occasional art prints. The artwork was all of one particular theme; nudes, female nudes. Heavy velour curtains hung full-length to the floor and were drawn tight against the outside world, blocking out any natural light.

Familiarization complete, Felicity looked back to Audrey. The woman had perched herself on the arm of one of the sofas. Audrey dismissed them both with a wave of a hand. 'Towels in the usual place Terry. You know where the bathroom is. We'll catch up later.'

******

Terry led Felicity back in to the hallway. He chirped away as they walked up the hall. Felicity's nerves settled a little. A young woman appeared out of a side room almost colliding with them. Felicity noticed that she was bare foot. Her small frame was well covered in an oversize sweatshirt but despite the unflattering covering Felicity could see that the girl had small boobs.

She cracked a smile at Felicity. 'Hi Terry.' She winked at him. 'Have you been shopping again?' The girl did not wait for an answer but turned in to another room further along the hall. Terry ignored the girl's comment. 'Here we are Felicity.'

He grabbed her a towel from an airing cupboard and opened the door to the bathroom. Felicity stuck her head in and felt the wet heat of a bath recently used. The fog was moist and soapy; luxuriant and inviting.

'I'll be around. Come find me when you're done. We'll have a cuppa.' He gave her a reassuring grin then reached down to change a sign that hung on the door handle from 'free' to 'in use'. Felicity shut the door behind her and quickly noticed that there was no lock on the inside.

A sense of desperation enabled her to console herself with the fact that the sign would have to suffice. She pulled off the heavy work boots, wincing as she viewed the state her feet were in. Her feet were now so sore that she had grown accustomed to the discomfort, it had become almost irrelevant, but seeing them in such a state scared her.

She hung the heavy coat on the back of the door and stripped down to her knickers, she grimaced as she caught a pungent waft of fishy odour. She threw them in to the tub. They could be washed while she washed. She left the remainder of her soiled clothing in a heap on the floor by the door, a makeshift door wedge. It was a horrible thought that she would have to put it all back on but at least she could be clean for a while. She climbed in to the bathtub. She turned the shower controls releasing a steady jet of hot water in to the bath. She stepped in pulling the shower curtain across as she did. The hot water stung her feet and she had difficulty remaining at first but she stayed there until the initial burst of pain subsided. The shower flow was firm and she allowed herself to stand for a while enjoying the massaging effect on her head, neck and shoulders. She felt the grime, both material and metaphorical, rinse from her hair and skin. She opened her mouth allowing the needles of water to cleanse inside. She found a bar of soap on a rope hanging from the shower controls. She caked herself in lather, breathed in the heady scent. She trod her underwear in to the flowing suds until the cotton looked clean enough. When she drew back the shower curtain the bathroom was enveloped in a mist. Felicity leant across the sink to open the window but found it impossible to open. The lever moved and the stay could be released but try as she did, she could not budge it. She looked more closely and spotted the faint impression of slotted screw heads. Someone had screwed the window frames shut and painted over them. She shrugged, a security measure maybe? She toweled herself off.

She wrung the knickers out as hard as she could, still too wet to put back on she tucked them in to one of the big coat pockets. No knickers for a while. With great reluctance she dressed back in to her old clothes and tugged the too-big boots back on to her much cleaner but still sore feet. She eased open the door and found the hallway empty. She could hear the feint sound of music further on up the hall but otherwise nothing. Politely, she folded the towel leaving it on the side of the bath and decided to find Terry. She surmised that Terry may be waiting for her back in the lounge so she headed back up the hallway. As she approached, she heard the woman's voice. Audrey was talking sharply.

Felicity did not mean to pry but it was difficult not to. The house was quiet but for the music she had just heard. What was clear was that Audrey's tone had changed. She now spoke as if discussing plans. It could even have been described as conspiratorial.

Felicity stopped just short of the lounge door taking care not to be seen and continued to listen. She frowned as she heard Terry respond.

'I think she's ripe Audrey, I really do.'

Audrey chuckled at his insistence. 'Well, I can see why you like her Terry that's for sure! Just got to ensure that we get her on-board quick. I can think of a few that would be interested, she's got the look so there's no denying that she would be an asset.'

'I think we could get her hooked up quite easily. It didn't take much to get her to come here with me, did it?' Terry convinced. 'She's pretty naïve, that I can tell you!'

'Very true.' Audrey conceded. 'You're a persuasive little bugger, I'll give you that. Of course, you'll get sorted as usual. I'll give Macca a call. He'll help us get her in shape. I'll do it now in fact. Strike while the iron's hot as they say.'

'Time and tide wait for no man!' Terry chuckled.

Audrey laughed. 'Or woman!'

Felicity listened as the telephone receiver was lifted. Audrey gave Terry directions. 'Go and check in on her Terry. Make sure she's comfortable. We'll sort her somewhere to sleep until Macca can get over. Be careful not to spook her. Okay?'

'I'll sort it Audrey.'

Felicity turned quickly and sprinted to the far end of the hallway. She felt so unsettled, her gut was twisting and she had learnt to listen to it. The music she had heard earlier was now much louder, she was closer to its source. It was coming from one of the rooms nearby. She was starting to feel the identifiable signs of panic welling up inside her. She knew something was not right.

She eyed each door with urgency, she had to take a chance on which room to dart in. She needed some time, some space, a moment at least to collect herself and to decide what to do next. She had not liked the tone of the conversation between Terry and Audrey and though she could not be certain, she was almost certain that they had been referring to her. To what ends, she could not even begin to consider. Asset? Ripe? Shape? What did it all mean?

Her stomach lurched as she heard Terry step in to the hallway, calling out to Audrey. 'Back in a minute. I'll see if one of the girls has some clobber she can borrow.'

Felicity shoved the nearest door open, desperation fueling her every move. Nothing could have prepared her for the sight that she was confronted with.

Chicken-like legs barely supported the man's gelatinous upper body. His flabby white gut wobbled and slapped in rhythmic waves with each vulgar thrust of his hips. A mat of dark dense hair covered his chest, another cloaked his upper back and spread down in to the small of his back, the hair was rooted like thick, damp moss, that spread down to his saggy arse cheeks.

Perspiration smeared his brow, beads of clammy sweat dripped off his nose, ran down his belly then dropped off on to the smooth blemish-free bottom of a young girl.

The girl, impaled, was bent over double in front of him, her fingers pressed hard into the top of her skinny pale feet, an effort to withstand his ugly thrusts. Her eyes were shut tight, grimacing, discomfort etched across her face. She was tiny, a fact all the more exaggerated by the man's heavy frame. Her hair was short and dark. Her boobs small mounds on her own lithe frame, limbs slim, it was hard to age her, she was young possibly adolescent.

His eyes were locked in, wide open in lust, focused only on the image in the dressing table mirror opposite. The man remained engrossed, oblivious to Felicity's presence in the room.

White powder dusted the top of the bedside cabinet. A rolled-up bank note was sat discarded among the snow. A radio on the bedside cabinet was blaring tinny pop music.

The hastily opened door let a waft of draught in that swept across the girl's skinny neck. Her eyes popped open and she spotted Felicity standing in the doorway. 'Fucking hell!'

The girl's startled yelp halted the man's thrusting. Angered by the uninvited intrusion, he bellowed. 'What the fuck?!'

'Jesus!' Hollered Terry in response. He had just entered the doorway behind Felicity. Instinctively, he reached out and gripped her shoulder. She spun, fast and hard. A violent reaction to his unwelcome touch. Her pointy elbow swooped up in a near perfect arc of destructive force and smashed in to his ratty nose. The damage was significant. His hands flung up to the injury. A long, drawn-out scream of anguish turned to a gurgle as the crimson flood cascading from his nostrils entered his mouth. He was a proper bleeder. Triggered, Felicity really let fly, the steel toecap of her right boot thudding into Terry's balls sending him to the floor in a bloodied bawling heap. She kicked again at the back of his unprotected head, relishing the crack she heard as his skull splinter on impact.

Now in full flow, she turned to face the fat man. He was frozen to the spot, his jaw wide open in shock. There was no attempt to cover himself, to hide his shame. He stood shaking like a sweaty bowl of vanilla blancmange. The girl had dropped to the floor and had crawled over to a corner where she curled, fetus-like, her arms and hands enveloping her head, trying block out the horror show that was happening around her.

Felicity stabbed an accusing finger towards the man's round face. 'You! You are a fucking pervert!' Spittle from her vent flecked his blood-drained face. She clawed at his face causing him to fall backwards on to the bed whimpering. The sudden appearance of Audrey saved him from immediate retribution. 'You little bitch!' Audrey hissed.

Felicity turned quickly and immediately spotted the kitchen knife in the woman's hand.

'I'll fuckin' gut you like a pig!'

Audrey shot towards Felicity with menacing intent but she was no match for Felicity's youth. In a flash Felicity wrenched the radio from the top of the cabinet, tearing the wire free from the plug socket and slammed it in to the side of Audrey's head. The radio split open spewing its electrical guts, the innards dangled like tentacles from the casing. A gash, deep and long, spread across the side of Audrey's cheek bone. The woman's candy floss hair became streaked with bright, sticky blood. The woman froze, open-mouthed, stunned. Felicity swung again, quick and fast before the knife could be brought in to play. The jagged remnants of the plastic radio casing gouged in to Audrey's face tearing in to her eye, hooking it and uprooting it. Audrey screamed in agony dropping to her knees, the knife dropping from her hand as she reached to her mangled eye socket, her eyeball now dangling useless from the hole in her face. Felicity dropped the carcass of the radio down on top of the woman's head and fled.

Without a glance backwards, she was quickly through the hallway, ignoring the girls and punters that now appeared, popping their heads out of doorways to see what all the commotion was about. As she left a car pulled in to the curb. Ominous looking, clearly expensive, diamond-white paintwork with tinted windows. She dared not hang around despite her curiosity. When she heard the clunk of opening car doors, she only concerned herself with putting distance between herself and the building.

It was some time before she felt confident enough to allow her pace to slow. Adrenalin had served her well but she was knackered. Her hands were shaking, gazing down at them she noticed the were caked in a crust of drying blood. It had got under her finger nails and on to her t-shirt too. She cursed as she realized that she had left the big coat on the back of the bathroom door and with it, nestling damp in the pocket; her knickers.

Despite these things, she felt no remorse, she felt something for sure but it was certainly neither regret nor remorse. She was lightheaded, energized, she was actually buzzing. She felt exultant, triumphant. The violence she had administered was completely justified in her mind. Being the one who controlled the pain and who should feel it felt absolutely right. She realized she was panting and made a conscious effort to control her breathing. What she did know was that she needed to get cleaned up again. The only issue was that she had no idea of where she was or where any facilities might be. So, with no other plan, she walked again.

VII

When the road she walked intersected with other roads she would sensibly look up at the street signs; some of them ornately embossed, fixed high up on the buildings. She had no idea where she was but as she came across another intersection, she recognised one particular street name, 'Oxford Street', 'city of Westminster, W1'. She knew most of the most famous London street names and if she was not wholly familiar with them she was, at least, familiar enough that she could relate them to some piece of historical or cultural information she had read about. She had developed a strong interest in London culture, history and geography. She had read just about every book on the subject she had loaned from the mobile library that visited the home. But in her wildest dreams, she had certainly never envisaged herself standing where she was at that moment.

She had turned in off Tottenham Court Road junction in to the enormous thoroughfare. Flanked high on both sides with tall buildings, many of which housed huge retail stores of the like she had never seen, its width offered a grandiosity that she had only seen in books. Double decker buses with open platforms at the back, conductors clinging to the pole, chugged noisily along its length and fat black cabs performed long drawn-out U-turns as and when they felt like it, much to the annoyance of other road users. Shoppers and tourists, crossed backwards and forwards across the road, slipping in and out of store entrances, their arms laden with bags advertising their recent patronages. Impatient drivers honked horns at the jaywalkers that stepped off the curb unannounced. The length and breadth of Oxford Street quite simply took her breath away.

She stopped and allowed herself to drink in its splendour. All her earlier experiences were soon forgotten amid a flood of sights, sounds and smells. She gawped in amazement at the elderly gentleman, small round glasses and peaked cap suggesting a revolutionary, carrying a tall banner that expressed; 'Less passion from less protein: Less fish meat bird cheese egg: Peas beans nuts and sitting'

She passed a street stall festooned with souvenir tack at tourist prices, a plethora of red, white and blue. She browsed its stock of union flags, keyrings, ornaments, stickers, snow globes and weird-looking little dolls encased in clear cylindrical tubes dressed in a variety of traditional British costume. T-shirts dangled from hangers, high and out of reach, above those packaged tightly in squares on a rack below; 'My sister went to London and all I got was a lousy t-shirt'.

She ran her hand over the front of her own crusty, holed and stinky top. She picked at a scab of dried blood, no longer able to recognise the colour it had originally been.

The stallholders were hustling; attentive and focused on the flow of human traffic that passed. They called to tourists in their strong London accents exhorting their wares, encouraging them to spend their exchanged currency. To them, she was just another anonymous person, a body on the street. They did not award her a second glance. Felicity was invisible to them and that was why she waited at a sensible distance, careful not to arouse suspicion. And her patience paid off. As both of the stall holders became embroiled in negotiations with punters she swooped. As she quickly passed back across the stall's frontage, her small nimble fingers dived and liberated one of the square packages below the dangling t-shirts. She was swiftly away with her prize. She was careful not to cause a disturbance as she hurried away but upped her pace just enough to put space between her and the stall. Within moments her getaway was thwarted as she stumbled in to an impenetrable swarm exiting Oxford Circus underground station.

If she was being pursued by angry stallholders she dared not look. She ducked low and forced her way in to the crowd, burrowing deep, desperate to find a way through. 'Oi! Manners!' Reprimand came as she weaved her way in. A stiff elbow told her to watch how she went. A good shove from another traveler reminded her again, the effort almost throwing her off balance. She righted herself quickly. A trampling underfoot would not be a good way to die. Any sense of direction was soon lost in the crowd. The pressure, the human heat, made her claustrophobic. There were moments when she felt herself lifted, her legs bicycling as she scrabbled madly with her booted feet, searching for purchase with the pavement. She was caught off-guard as another disgruntled barge sent her crabbing sideways. It was a bitter sweet incident. Her pride may have been slightly dented but the momentum had aided her passage through the crowd. She squeezed out like a squeaky fart.

Safe from a citizen's arrest and a proper hiding, she bent, hands on her knees, regaining her composure. Then she looked around and found herself in Argyle Street. It was a no-through road for vehicles blocked to traffic from Oxford Street. Turning in to the street it was as if she had gone backwards in time. Once again, she found herself engulfed in another swarm of human life, only this time they came piling out of the tube station from a side exit. This time she was swimming against the majority of the tide as the travelers mostly turned back up towards Oxford Street. She fought hard against the flow, head down, leaning forward, pushing back against the hoard that threatened to force her back the way she had come. At last, she got through. Out in to a wide cosmopolitan street.

Eateries selling take away pizza slices and filled baguettes opened out on to the street, alongside restaurants boasting huge glass frontages for those that could afford to dine there. 'The Palladium theatre', an imposing building with wide steps flanked by tall pillars commanded a good part of the street. The main entrance itself was crowned by an extravagantly designed apex; a vision of grandeur.

Felicity relaxed and enjoyed the sights, now confident that she was not being pursued. She stopped briefly to read the show poster outside the theatre. Here the pace seemed slower, less frenetic. Folk around her were more relaxed, socializing, like herself, enjoying the sights. She wandered on to where the street came to an end at a T-junction. A building across from the junction spoke of a different era. Its construction boasted a façade of black timber struts, ornate windows and white plasterwork, much like the Tudor houses she had seen in her history books. Above the buildings main entrance, large lettering spelled out; 'Liberty'. She noticed a post topped with direction signs clearly intended for tourists.

She was well and truly in the lap of the gods. When she had executed her plan to run from the home, she had only set her sights on getting to London. What she had not given any thought to, was where her final destination would be. She had no plan of action for her arrival in the big smoke. At that moment, she was surviving purely on her wits, guile and tenacity. Spotting the tourist signs was a small piece of luck. It lifted her spirits to see that the sign pointed her in the direction of public toilets. At least she could give herself a spruce up and change in to the fresh t-shirt there. After that she would regroup and consider her options. If she had none, she would have to make some. With her current priorities being a shit, a piss and a general tidy up she headed for the toilets. Making her way across a zebra crossing, she found them easily enough. They were located at a yawning urban estuary that fed in to another busy street. It was a street unlike any she had encountered before. There was no access to vehicles, at least, not at the end she stood. The street had been pedestrianized.

But she had got distracted again. It was a common happening for her. Her curiosity always drawn to the new, the unusual, the interesting and the creative. But she needed to stick to her plans. Regaining focus, she headed towards the beckoning public facilities. She was surprised to find that the entrance was a flight of stairs flanked with aluminum railings that led down to subterranean facilities.

Though She had not felt particularly down or miserable, her thoughts and energy having been focused on survival, she felt a sense of achievement in having found her way without being picked up, arrested, hurt seriously or killed. Now she was looking forward to the opportunity for some long-overdue ablutions. Her celebration was unfortunately brief as a barrier dropped down to block her way to the toilets.

'What's the password?'

Felicity frowned confused at the arm that now blocked her way. Her confusion quickly morphed in to irritation. She had come a long way, overcome some pretty challenging hurdles and was now desperate for the loo. She looked up ready to challenge the owner of the appendage and was startled. Her eyes widened at the young punk's shock of lurid green hair. A work of art that had somehow been painstakingly teased and firmed upright in to dozens of individual spikes. His pierced earlobes were decorated with dangling silver crosses. A heavy dog chain hung from around his neck. His teeth were in poor health, some merely stumps, the others greyer than tombstones. He smelled of sick.

Felicity gave his arm a gentle push but he stepped in closer blocking her way through.

'I need to go to the toilet.' She was annoyed with how pitiful she sounded but it was true. She eyed up the punk's tatty t-shirt. His appearance seemed somehow deliberate, a thought-through statement of anti-fashion, whereas her own she could boast was more authentic, a creation of some genuinely tough times. Ripped off sleeves, a crude DIY alteration, showed off his spotty shoulders and his miniscule collection of amateur tattoos, a big anarchy symbol and an indecipherable blur of a name. Sick boy grinned at her discomfort.

'That's not the password, darling. Try again!'

Another cohort chuckled at Sick boy's antics. Felicity looked over Sick boy's scrawny shoulder. Another mane of hair, stiff and bleached to within an inch of its life, was cut in to a mohawk hairstyle. The sides of the head were shaved leaving a narrow blade of sculptured hair that ran in a strip from the punk's forehead all the way back to the nape of his neck. From root to tip, the height of this creation was a good six inches. A silver ring swung from his septum.

The third punk had chosen a less labour-intensive coiffure, easy mainte-nance over grandiose gesture. He wore very short cropped, hair dyed jet black, so black that it was clearly unnatural. In the middle of his forehead, he had tattooed a simple inverted cross, the blue Indian-ink had begun to spread.

Felicity barked. 'I really need to go. Can you move please?'

But Sick boy was having too much fun. Unblinking, he widened his eyes, twisting his features closer to her face. He snarled. 'If you knew the password it wouldn't be a problem but you clearly don't and we can see you're new around her, so in the interest of hospitality, I think we can come to an arrange-ment.' He offered his palm. 'Grease my palm with silver and we can overlook the fact that you've forgotten the password.'

'Forgotten it! I didn't know it in the first place.' Felicity spat. 'Listen, I've got no money and I don't know your stupid password, so can you move? Now!'

Surprised by Felicity's pluck sick boy feigned shock. 'Well,' he said to no one in particular, 'How rude! To think we were trying to be helpful. What do you think lads?' He looked at his friends in mock conference before turning back to her. 'You see, darling, I was going to give you a break but as you've been so rude to me and my friends here, I think you should find somewhere else to have a shit or change your jam rag or whatever. This convenience is now closed.'

Felicity had had all she was willing to put up with. She was now well overdue to go to the toilet and her urgency was threatening to embarrass her. She grasped his forearm strongly. She was surprised. Despite the punk's skinny frame, the man possessed a wiry strength. She grunted with effort which made the group laugh all the more. She would not let them make her look weak. She would not beg or cry.

With heavy capitulation, she released his arm. She pondered her options. Should she launch a full-bloodied assault on the man? This would without doubt cause a huge ruckus and result in unwelcome attentions and possible arrest. Or she could call it day, move on and try to find a discreet passage in which she could relieve her burgeoning passages. Before she could decide, a voice, female, cut the tension. 'Oh, for fucks sake Minty! Leave the girl alone will you!'

Startled, Sickboy Minty dropped his arm. 'Jesus, Mel, we were only having a laugh!'

Felicity turned to the source of the voice. The sight was like a full stop, darker than dark. Black fitted the description but it was ghostly black. Voluminous, frizzy hair spun black from her head. It would have been harder to find a deeper black. Her clothes were black, shades of black admittedly but black all the same. A black biker jacket, custom decorated with studs and stars, covered a black string top over a washed-out black t-shirt. At her waist, an amazing belt. Made from dozens of brass bullet casings it hung loosely from her hip to her upper thigh on the opposite leg like a machine gunner's belt. It was like nothing she had seen before. She raised her eyes in curiosity, eager to see the mouth of the voice. It was not a disappointment. Strongly made up, the girl's pale complexion was almost white, this added effect drawing out her eyes and lips, making them all the more prominent. It was a look for a well-practiced, dedicated hand. One that gave the impression of many hours spent creating the eye make-up that decorated her eyes and the definition that reddened her lips. Her eye make-up was black as coal and sharp, developing in to points that veered away towards her temples. The effect was stunning. Rather than darkening her eyes and throwing them in to shade, her artistry lifted them, accentuating the whites and bringing out the green of her irises.

A gurgle in her gut reminded her of why she was at the top of the stairs. With urgency, she nodded a quick 'Thank you' in the girl's direction and hurtled down the stairs as fast as was safe to do so.

The facilities were incredibly busy. The cubicles were like a merry-go-round of constant use, doors being swung open and slammed shut in equal measure. Luckily, she was able to dart in to a vacant cubicle before her discomfort turned to embarrassment.

Suitably relieved she approached the wash basins. She was aware of others moving around her but no one seemed to pay her any attention. Unfortunately, there was no soap. It was kick in the fanny but at least she had running water and she could change out of the wreck of a t-shirt she was wearing. A change of trousers would have been nice, her cords were grimy and stiff, but she would have to stick with them for the time being. She pulled her top up and over her shoulders. Welts, bruises and scratches marked her limbs. Her small bra had also seen better days. Lifting her arms, she winced at the smell. Her armpit hair was knotted and smelly. She looked at her appearance in the full-width mirror that spanned the row of sinks. It told a sorry story.

Running the taps, she thrust the old t-shirt under the water for some time, scrunching and twisting the rag to agitate the dirt so that some of it would wash out. The water ran brown down the plug hole. After some minutes of effort, the top began to soften and the water began to run clearer. Felicity used the garment as a wash cloth to wipe as much of the grime off her upper body as she could. When satisfied that she could do all she had done she looked over her shoulder to see if a cubicle was free. She was contemplating using one to strip her lower body to clean her privates.

A door swung open and the girl appeared. She adjusted the bullet belt and joined Felicity by the basins. Felicity fiddled awkwardly with the sodden rag of a t-shirt.

'Woah! You've seen better days.' The girl looked her over. 'And so, has that fuckin' t-shirt!'

The comments made Felicity defensive. 'It's fine, I've got a new one.' Felicity showed her the stolen t-shirt, still tucked in its cellophane wrapping.

The girl raised her eyebrows. 'Nice choice!' she jested. Felicity's skin tightened, self-conscious and awkward. 'Hey, it's cool. Plenty of runaways pass through here.'

'I'm not a runaway!' Felicity snapped back, a little too urgently.

'My mistake.' She eased her satchel off her shoulder and rummaged in the bag. She pulled out a tube of liquid eye liner. She paused a moment, then reached back inside. She handed Felicity an aerosol deodorant. 'Here, you can use this.' The girl made no eye contact but continued to hold it out for her to take. Felicity swallowed her pride; it was all she had left. She reached out and took the can from her hand. Their fingers touched.

'Thanks.'

'No problem.' The girl removed the eyeliner from its tube and focused her attention on the mirror.

Felicity watched intently as the girl re-defined the wings around her eyes, her technique was well-practiced and concise. She popped the eyeliner back in its tube and checked her lipstick with her little finger. 'Girl's got to keep up her appearances!'

Despite her awkwardness, Felicity smiled at Mel's antics.

'That's better, girl.' She smiled back at her. 'Listen, don't worry about them dickheads up there. They're always hanging around and getting up to stuff. They're harmless really.' She nodded at the deodorant still in Felicity's hand. 'You gonna use that then?' She gave a laugh. 'I would if I were you!'

******

The two girls stepped out of the public toilets together. Felicity disposed of the remnants of her old t-shirt in a bin.

'Name's Mel by the way.'

'Felicity.'

'Proper lovely name that! Pleased to meet you, Felicity.'

Mel strode confidently back in to the street. It was obvious that she knew the place well. The three punk boys were now busy hamming it up for a couple of Japanese tourists, clambering over each other and generally fooling around for the camera while they took holiday snaps.

'Consumerism at its best!' Mel gave a short belly grunt. 'The punters get their pics and the boys get their quid.' Felicity watched as the tourists handed the boys a pound note for their services rendered.

There seemed to be more youths gathered around than she remembered. It could have been that she had been focused on getting in to the toilets and had not noticed. Mel stopped to talk to a couple of boys. Felicity stood back out of the way, shuffling awkwardly on the spot, toeing the paving. Seeing herself in the mirror back in the public toilets had made her conscious about her appearance and she felt conspicuous.

The boys speaking to Mel wore heavy boots, made of leather the colour of oxblood. Their blue jeans were turned up short showing a lot of their ankles. Over-long boot laces were wrapped around the leather and tied through a loop at the rear. Both their heads were cropped, one of which was barely a dark shadow. Both sucked on cigarettes held palm in as they chatted. They were well acquainted and there was laughter among the three.

Dark shadow boy wore a black polo shirt, three buttons, top one undone, with a bright yellow striped collar and laurel wreath detail to his left breast. His friend was wearing a simple 'grandad' collar t-shirt, off-white, ribbed with a short row of buttons up to a collarless neck. Narrow red elastic braces clipped on to the waist band of his jeans ran up to his shoulders. He had his non-smoking hand thrust in to the front pocket of his jeans to take the pressure off his balls.

It was a warm sunny day and a menagerie of human life had congregated in the area, milling about and catching up. Mel broke away from the boys and returned to Felicity. 'Listen. I don't know what plans you've got but I'm gonna take a chance and say your diary is empty.' Mel put her hand on Felicity's shoulder.

'How about you stick with me for a bit? I'll look after you.'

Felicity let the girl's hand rest there. She was surprised that she felt comfortable with it. She could call it instinct but for some reason she trusted Mel.

'Listen Flick,' She looked around. 'I don't like the idea of you being on your own around here tonight. How about you come back to my pad for a bit. We can get something to eat and I've got plenty of clobber that I can lend you to wear.' Remembering her comment back by the sinks in the toilets that had triggered Felicity's fragile pride, she added, 'until you get your own stuff obviously.'

The shortening of her 'proper lovely name' had taken Felicity aback somewhat but she quite liked it. It felt familiar and friendly. Flick.

Since getting tidied up, she had not had a minute to consider what she was going to do next. At that moment, stood with Mel and the two skinheads she had very few options. None of them very palatable. Her experiences so far had taught her not to drop her guard, to be suspicious and to give away very little about herself but something about Mel made her feel safe.

She did allow herself some reservations. What if it was a ruse to get her somewhere she didn't want to be? like before, with Ratboy? Maybe she was better off on her own.

'Absolutely no pressure Flick but we've got a bathroom and I've got a bean casserole stewing for dinner that we can share.'

What if Mel's offer was genuine? What if she could get clean and fed without the risk of being maimed in her efforts to do so? What if Mel was offering sanctuary?

She weighed it up. She felt confident, that if needed, she could take Mel in straight fist fight. She took a breath and went with her hungry, gnawing, empty gut.

'Sounds like heaven.'

VIII

Mel took Felicity by the hand, pulling her along, encouraging her to follow her. They entered beneath the arch of 'Carnaby street' into a vibrant festival of colour and activity. Tourists wandered along, free of traffic, exploring the sights of one of the most famous streets in London's contemporary history, while on many corners gathered, as had become the norm, the different tribes of Britain's youth.

The Shakespeares Head public house on the first corner was doing well due to the good weather. Wooden picnic tables scattered around its perimeter were crammed with glasses and bottles. The patrons perched on the seating cross-legged, talking animatedly while waving long, filtered cigarettes. Next to the pub, a small side road, Fouberts place, ran off the Carnaby. Its way was peppered with small boutiques that seemed to cater for particular tribes. Windows were full of clothing and shoes, the shop signs resplendent with union flags. 'The Cavern' catered for the mod revivalists. Placards and display boards plastered with button badges and sew-on patches spilled from the stores. Bright scarves and bags hung motionless, no wind to make them flutter or sway, alongside an abundance of different styles of headwear; get a hat get ahead.

On another corner, a high building, its lower level painted in an eye-catching red highlighting broad windows crammed with pop-art footwear fit for the new modernists, blasted the revivalist champions; The Jam, from its sound system. Felicity looked up at the garish yellow store sign; Melanddi.

'To be someone must be a wonderful thing.'

A group of youths huddled around a lone scooter. A boating blazer, brightly striped, hung like a flag over the shoulder of one white trousered troubadour. A girl, doll-like, her hair shiny in the sun and cut in to a Sassoon bob, sat side saddle on the scooter seat. Her ski pant leggings held crisp and tight by flat soled lace up pumps.

'A famous footballer a rock singer'

'Or a big film star'

Yes, I think I would like that

Further along, Rock Dreams, a music store, filled the street with the sound of romance, new romance.

'Don't you want me baby?'

'Don't you want me? Ooooh.'

Distracted once again, Felicity stopped to gawp at the kaleidoscope of album covers in the window.

'C'mon Flick, we've got a bus to catch.' Mel tugged her arm good -naturedly.

They had walked its length, arriving at another T-section where the Carnaby carnival ended and Beak Street started. Left they went for a few yards, Mel on autopilot, before darting down Golden Square. They moved too quickly for Felicity to take in all that she wanted to but passed tailors windows festooned with a sea of exquisite cloth, glass-doored offices flanked with big-leafed imitation plants in huge pots, doorways with pinned cards that offered 'models' and 'massage'. Felicity felt her stomach flip at the reminder.

Past Golden Square gardens, where homeless folk and alcoholics, familiar to her after her encounter with the tramp, hogged the benches they crossed over Brewer Street past the Vintage Magazine store, its main window rammed tight with a vast variety of used magazines and booklets available within. Elaborate prints and posters relating to films, music and the arts created a vibrant backdrop. The shop offered thousands of photographic reprints, posters and other ephemera of film, pop, TV stars and pin-ups to browse and purchase.

On they travelled in to the last leg of Denman Street, Soho, full of eateries and restaurants. A road that veered left before popping them out, on to the main road through Piccadilly. Mel led them both to a bus stop where, at last, Felicity could rest.

She was flushed with the pace. Having not eaten for a very long time, she was starting to feel the adverse effects. Fatigued and running on empty, she struggled to remain standing on her wobbly legs. Her head began to swim, her vision blurring. Instinctively she grasped at Mel, fingertips clutching at her studded jacket with desperation. Mel grabbed her before she fell. Her expression one of concern 'Oh, Flick! I'm so sorry!'

She turned Felicity's slender frame, helping her lean against the bus shelter. Happy that she was well enough supported she rooted around in her satchel with her free hand. 'I do that run so often I forget what a trek it can be.' Mel retrieved the mangled remnants of a kit-kat from the bottom of her satchel. She slid the two-finger chocolate bar from its wrapper and handed it to Felicity. 'My emergency supplies.' She licked chocolate off her fingers.

Felicity chewed quickly and the sweet energy hit her instantly, the insides of her mouth tingled with the richness of the milk chocolate. She offered an embarrassed smile. 'You looked like you were gonna carp it!' Mel laughed.

They did not have to wait long. Double deckers stopped frequently, Mel quickly checking different numbers and destinations as they pulled in loading and unloading their human cargo. Mel spotted their ride; she gave quick instructions. 'Upstairs, as close to the front as we can get. Hopefully the conductor won't have got to us by the time we get home!'

Encouraged by Mel shoving her from behind, she gripped the pole and pulled herself up on to the back platform. They climbed the curving narrow stairs and walked the gangway. She grabbed the back of a seat for balance as the bus pulled away from the stop, the floor throbbing with the engines roar. Mel stayed close, ushering her towards the front of the bus where they found a two-seater free. Mel let her sit next to the window. A sliding mechanism allowed passengers to open the top portion of the window to let air in. It seemed that the upper level of the bus was a sanctuary for cigarette smokers and many of the passengers on board were happily puffing away. Felicity reached up and slid the window open.

Mel sat her satchel on her lap and pulled out a packet of cigarettes, consulate. Felicity wondered if the satchel was like some sort of Tardis, the number of items that Mel seemed to have stored in there was fascinating. She watched as Mel pulled out a cigarette and tucked it between her red lips. A feint waft of mint was replaced by the pungent odour of Sulphur as Mel struck a match. She lit the cigarette and dropped the box of matches back in to her satchel, the ship logo sinking below to the depths. Felicity had never smoked and the second-hand smoke aggravated her throat, making it itch. She gave a low cough.

'Sorry Flick. Should have offered you one.' Mel held out the pack.

'Thanks, but I don't smoke.' Felicity explained further. 'I've never smoked. Never had the opportunity to be honest.'

Felicity stared out of the front window of the bus. High up and as wide as the bus, it offered a panoramic view of the journey. It was a great view, a great experience. She had never been on a double decker bus before. After all the incident and chaos of the last few hours she was just happy to sit and let the world pass by the window for a bit.

'C'mon up,' Mel led the way as she had done since they had met earlier that day. 'I'll show you where I kip.' Felicity followed close behind as the pair climbed the wooden staircase to the first floor of the house. It was an effort to climb the stairs, they felt odd. Her thighs complained as she fought against the abnormal lean that the staircase had adopted due to settlement. She placed a hand on the bare, graffiti-scrawled wall to steady herself. Holes in the wall's plaster exposed ribs of timber lathes. The flight led on to a long landing that split back to front of the house. It was carpeted with the remnants of what had clearly been an expensive wool carpet. Deep red with ornate scrollwork, the hessian backing now peered through the carpets most worn areas. Mel caught Felicity looking.

'We rescued that from a skip outside the Three Bells pub. They were having a refurb. Makes the place a bit warmer don't you think?'

Felicity nodded in distracted agreement. Her attention had been grabbed by noise coming from a door that had been left slightly ajar. It was music. Music so hard, so aggressive, so attacking, that it would have been impossible to ignore. It was quite unlike anything she had heard before. Its structure sounded simple, to the point, with buzzsaw guitars and street-level vocals. It was a furious sound.

'Cause I can't stand the peace and quiet.'

'All I want is a running riot.'

Curiosity drew Felicity to the gap in the door. Mel explained.

'That's Quiet.'

'Quiet? How much louder could it be?' Things were just getting odder by the minute.

Mel grinned. 'No, you daft cow, that's Quiet's space. His room. We know him as Quiet. Peanut gave him that nickname when he first turned up. He didn't say a lot and tended to keep himself to himself so Peanut called him Quiet. It stuck, obviously. He's a nice bloke to be fair, just needed to get know us I suppose!' Mel approached the door and rapped hard on the paneling. 'I'll introduce you!' As if on a spring the door slammed shut with an almighty bang. 'Think Quiet wants a quiet night in!' She grinned 'Unsociable git!' She said it loud knowing he would hear.

'C'mon space cadet, follow me to my humble abode.' Mel led on towards the rear of the house to a door at the far end. A shoot bolt, a sturdy piece of hardware more suited to a shed door, provided security. The whole mechanism being secured by a padlock. Using a key attached to a lace around her neck she let herself in. 'Not foolproof but should hopefully slow any fucker up that tries to get in.' She explained. 'Ain't got much worth nicking but it's the space I need protecting.'

The room was small. Not much larger than a box room at best. There was a mattress covering most of the floor with a sleeping bag laid neatly on top of it. The window was wide open making it chilly. Felicity turned to look back at the door and noticed that Mel had taken the precaution of fitting a second shoot bolt to the inside of the door. Mel noticed Felicity looking at it. 'Keeps the pervs out at night!' She chuckled.

She had flopped down on to the mattress and was tugging at her Dr Marten boots. 'Give us a hand.' She extended a leg. Felicity read the gesture and grabbed the heel and toe. She gave a yank causing Mel to slide off the mattress. Mel laughed heartily. 'Hold up! You'll bust a blood vessel! Let me get a grip.' Mel got a firmer grip on the mattress. This time the boot came off. Encouraged by Felicity's success, Mel shoved her other booted foot towards her. Once Mel had been de-booted Felicity removed her own oversized work boots. She plonked herself down next to Mel. She dabbed gingerly at her red-raw toes.

Mel was weighing one of the hefty work boots in her hands, her top lip curled up in distaste. 'Jeez! We'll need to get these sorted. These things must kill your feet!' She glanced down at Felicity's now bare feet. 'Fuckin' 'ell! State of your feet! They look wrecked. What happened?' Felicity curled her toes tight with embarrassment.

'I lost my shoes.' It was all she felt able to offer. She was not ready to give Mel the warts and all explanation.

Mel jumped up. 'Stay there.' She ordered as she darted from the room. Felicity had no plans to go anywhere. Not at that moment anyway. With Mel gone the room felt eerily sedate. Mel was a little fire cracker with enough energy to light a Christmas tree that was for sure but Felicity liked her already. She was exciting and dynamic, interesting. Mel was like no one she had ever met. She leant back on the mattress and gazed around the room. Patches of the walls were herniating, swollen from behind with crumbling lathe and plaster. Fissures, some big enough to squeeze a finger in to, cut across the high corners feeding thinner tributaries that trickled away to nothing. The woodchip wallpaper was doing a grand job of holding the hundred-year-old render together. Mel had personalized the room, band posters and Xeroxed gig flyers were stuck to the woodchip with sellotape, like makeshift sticking plasters. The names, the places, the bands were unfamiliar to her. Crass. Siouxsie and the banshees. Joy Division. Killing Joke.

The imagery of the flyers was as random and odd as the band names they advertised, moody, dark and controversial in an art-school kind of way. A thick coat of shit-brown gloss, like armour, coated the skirting boards. Yellowed Formica shelving, once gleaming white, had been put to good use by Mel. Her clothing was piled there creating a makeshift open-plan wardrobe, knickers, stockings, some t-shirts, couple of skirts, big baggy jumpers and skinny black jeans were stacked in neat little piles. Other clothing, too heavy for the shelves; her studded leather jacket, a long black trench coat, a military style parka hung from an old metal display rail. Another recycled item.

Mel seemed to use the lowest shelf as a dressing table, a free-standing mirror was propped up in the middle, flanked by hairbrushes, hairspray and an assortment of cosmetics. Mel clearly liked black. Felicity spotted a silver cassette player. She stood, keeping her balance as she trod across the springy mattress. She picked up the cosmetics, reading the small labels before replacing them. A brown case was kept closed by two clips. She pressed the clips and they popped open and she lifted the lid. The inside of the case held neat rows of cassettes; mostly home recorded with handwritten labels. She read the blurb on the spines and recognised some of the names she had seen on the walls of the room.

'Play one if you want.' Mel had returned bearing an armful of supplies, a blanket, toilet roll, a bottle of TCP.

Felicity was embarrassed. Though she had not meant to cause any harm or offence she knew that she should have asked permission before burrowing through Mel's belongings. 'Sorry, Mel.' Felicity fiddled awkwardly with the cassette case. 'I was just having a look.'

'Don't be daft, Flick, it's cool!' Mel dropped the items on to the bed joining her by the shelving. 'Pick one.' Felicity gazed at the labels for what seemed like an age until they all blurred in to one unreadable fuzz of biro.

'I don't know any of these bands.' She admitted.

Mel chuckled. 'It don't matter. Lucky dip it is then. Just close your eyes and pick one.'

Felicity closed her eyes, her fingertips rippling across the backs of the cassette boxes. She pulled one out. Mel took it from her and slipped it into the mouth of the player.

'Good choice!' Mel pushed the lip shut with a click. Felicity studied the track listing as Mel pressed the play button. Thirty seconds of tape hiss transformed, morphing in to instrumentation that was stark, stabbing electronica, a voice, deep and low, almost mournful broke in.

She read the band's name on the cassette card. 'Joy Division'

Mel was moving, her head bowed, her black back-combed hair stiff and unmoving, her arms in synchronization with her knee bends. She raised an arm and twirled it over her head as if spinning an invisible lasso. It was a moment of intense awkwardness for Felicity. She had danced before. Like a child. With the other kids in the home. It had been fun. But this felt different. Mel's gyrations looked sensual, somehow fitting the music perfectly. She wanted to join her in but was unsure how to.

And the sound was so new to her. It was so different to the pop music that they had listened to back at the home. The bassline was hypnotic and the singers' voice sounded like he was singing in a tunnel. Mel looked lost in the sound. Felicity was mesmerized by her abandonment in the moment.

'*Isolation*'

Mel stretched out a hand feeling for Felicity's own. Gentle and encouraging she moved Felicity's arm back and forth in time with the rhythm. Felicity found herself mimicking Mel's leg movements. Mel's face broke in to a grin. 'There you go! Now we're dancing Flick!'

'*Isolation*'

As the song played, they danced on. Felicity relaxed more and more until she too was lost in the moment, the crescendo rising until both of them were bouncing on the mattress and leaping around the room as one track ended and another began. They danced until the tape's small reels clattered to a begrudged halt leaving them both on their knees, breathless. A glow of perspiration across Mel's brow had snared a few strands of her jet-black hair, her winged eyeliner was moist and slipping. Felicity reached for Mel's forehead, gently she teased the hairs away from her warm, damp skin and lifted them back, up on to her head. Mel smiled at her then grabbed at the small brown bottle she had left lying forgotten on the floor. 'Here, let Nurse Mel have a look at them feet.'

Folding sheets of toilet paper into a pad then dampening it with the antiseptic liquid she wiped away the hours of dirt, grime and crusty blood from Felicity's wounded feet. She picked out the small fragments of gravel that had embedded themselves in the sole of her feet using a pair of tweezers. The liquid stung like hell, causing Felicity to wince. Mel chuckled and soothed in equal measures. The warm pain of the treatment only added to the warmth Felicity felt deep inside her gut. She was happier right then, at that moment, than she could remember ever having been.

******

The shared kitchen was at the rear of the old house. It boasted an electric hob, a sink and some storage cupboards. There was running cold water but no hot. Any hot water required had to be either boiled up in a kettle or on the hob.

Felicity did her best to be helpful as Mel heated up a bubbling pot of stew having earlier added soaked beans and pearl barley to the mix. A window spanned the breadth of the rear looking out over a scruffy garden. A lone tabby cat prowled among the foliage, stopping occasionally to peer up at the sparrows tantalizingly perched in the privet. Felicity turned back in to the kitchen as Mel spoke.

'We scrounge a lot of veg from the market when they finish up for the day. The stall holders just chuck it all in to piles as it won't last 'til next trading day.' Mel licked the wooden spoon before continuing to stir the pot. She reached for a pot of Marmite, adding a spoonful of to the pot. 'I haven't eaten meat for two years. It's hard sometimes but you get used to it.'

Mel, as was her way, knocked on fellow housemate's doors as they returned to her room. Calling through the door, to let others know that she had left the remainder warm on the hob if they were hungry. There was a lot of good-natured banter, Mel was clearly a kind soul and well liked. A chunky skinhead called Ronnie grabbed her and planted a smacker on her lips as he ran barefoot past them to the kitchen.

The lad's braces hung loosely around his buttocks. Felicity wondered why he bothered to wear braces if his jeans stayed up on their own. Mel shouted after him. 'Shit! I'll need another tetanus jab now!'

As they passed Quiet's door, Felicity noticed that it was closed tight and the music had stopped.

IX

Mel flicked off the side lamp and dropped back down on to the mattress. She had opened up the sleeping bag to double up as a quilt and scavenged a spare blanket from somewhere in the house. Laying alongside Felicity, she pulled the covers over them both and snuggled in to her own half, letting out long sigh. Then she turned and lay on her side facing the wall, curled, her knees drawn up.

Felicity had been taken aback when Mel had stripped to her knickers, unclipped her bra and jumped on to the mattress. Mel was clearly not fazed, some would even say she was uninhibited, but Felicity had not known where to look. Felicity lay on her back, eyes wide open. The stimulus of the day had revved her up and she was finding it difficult to come back down. She stared hard at the ceiling. The light from the moon bled through the makeshift curtain giving some illumination. She followed the cracks in the ceiling spidering away from the ceiling rose. A wispy, abandoned cobweb clung to the light bulb. She could feel the covers rise and fall with Mel's breathing.

She reached down for the hem of the t-shirt Mel had lent her and eased the garment up over her head. She turned slowly, carefully, on to her own side until she was almost spooning Mel. Mel's cloud of hair felt stiff and spiky in her face. The copious amount of hairspray she used to keep it that way made Felicity's nostrils itch, but she remained close, absorbing the warmth that Mel's bare torso was creating under the blankets. She edged even closer until she could tuck her knees behind Mel's own, appreciating the contact. She brought her hand up past Mel's hip and allowed it to drape gently across the girl's ribcage. Her own breathing quickened, she fought to control it. Her thoughts scrambled, her ears buzzed, blood rushed around her head as she caressed Mel's upper ribcage, her fingers as light as feathers. She ventured further, finding the lower curve of Mel's soft breast. She rested her hand there a moment before daring to cup her breast. Her fingers spread, feeling the baby-soft texture of her skin and the fullness of her breast. Her fingers roamed, exploring the area until she found Mel's erect nipple.

'What the fuck!' Mel jumped up like a stung cat. The lamp tumbled to the floor as Mel struck the switch.

Felicity squinted in the angry light; she clamped her hands to her eyes. When she moved her hands away, she found Mel kneeling close, a top clutched to her bosom, staring at her.

'Flick! What the fuck you playing at?'

Felicity took a moment to absorb the absurdity of the situation. Swimming in embarrassment, she struggled to look at the spiky-haired, pale-skinned girl clutching at her chest. She eased herself up to a sitting position. It was horribly awkward. She tried to explain. 'I'm not sure. I thought that maybe that's what you wanted?'

'Why on earth would you fuckin' think that Flick'?'

'I don't know Mel. I just thought,' she Paused, 'I just thought that you had been so good to me that, oh, I don't know, I wanted to be nice to you, like you've been to me.' She broke. 'I'm so sorry.' Her shoulders shuddered and she buried her face in her hands.

'Oh blimey, Flick I ain't like that. I just took a liking to you that's all.' She reached across and tried to pry Felicity's hands away. 'If you're that way, I ain't got a problem with it. It's okay honestly but it's not on offer.' Mel looked at Felicity apologetically. 'I like blokes.'

Felicity continued to clutch her face.

'Are you a lezzie flick?' It was a fair question considering what had happened.

Felicity dropped her hands. She sniffed hard. 'No.' She reached for the toilet roll. 'Well at least, I don't think so anyway.' Tears and snot hampered her ability to speak, she gurgled. She blew hard in to a wad of paper.

Mel lightened the atmosphere. 'How can you not know? It's simple, do you fancy boys or girls? Or maybe you like both?' She laughed. 'Have your cake and eat it!' Mel shivered, she unraveled her top and slipped it back over.

'Boys! I'm pretty sure I do anyway, I fancied Steve McQueen for a while, I even had a poster. I've never done nothing like this before.'

Mel began laughing harder. 'You are one confused bitch! Do you know that?'

Felicity smiled at Mel's laughter despite her fog of emotion. 'I suppose I am. Are you angry with me Mel?'

'Are you joking? This is the funniest thing that's happened to me for ages, you daft cow!'

Felicity flopped back on to the mattress. 'I am such an idiot.'

Mel reached over for her cigarettes. She plucked one from the packet and lit it. She took a long satisfying drag. She reached up to the window, shoving it wide open to let the cool night air in and to let the smoke out.

'Have you never had a boyfriend then?' She sat back down cross legged next to Felicity.

'No, never. We weren't allowed.' Felicity sighed. 'I did like a boy once, but we were really young, more friends really, maybe if we had been older, it may have developed into something but no. They were quite strict and watched us all the time.'

'What happened to him?' Mel asked.

'He went to a foster family and I never saw him again.' Felicity paused. 'I've never really thought about him until now. Kids came and went all the time. Especially the young ones.' Her blood ran cold as she realized that she was opening up to Mel, exposing herself. She remembered her little George, Georgina.

'We'll have to get you hooked up with a bloke then won't we. Can't have you grabbing me tit again, can I?' Mel grabbed a pillow and walloped Felicity around the head with it. She stood and stabbed her cigarette out on the window frame, flicking the butt out. She pulled the window closed.

'C'mon, let's get our heads down. Some of us need our beauty sleep!'

******

Felicity slept most of the following day. She was shattered both physically and mentally. It was Sunday which meant that Mel could be around. She looked after her, made her some food and left it by the mattress where Felicity found it, ate it and quickly fell back in to a deep slumber. Mel was concerned, Felicity hardly stirred and when she did, she was virtually incoherent. Mel decided to leave her sleeping, just checking in from time to time, resolved that rest would be the best thing if Flick was to recover from whatever ordeal she had experienced.

Felicity woke with a huge feeling of disorientation. Groggy, it took a moment to adjust her senses, to remember where she was. She began to relax as she recalled the events from the previous days. She heard the whistle of expelled air from Mel's nostrils as she slept alongside her and this helped to ground her. Felicity's shoulders were freezing. She reached for some cover and pulled it up over her goose-pimpled shoulder. Puffing heavily, she recognised the pressure of a full bladder. The overwhelming urge to wee slowly took precedence over her need for more shut eye. She had no idea what time it was. She tried mind over matter, she was so reluctant to get herself out of the cocoon she and Mel had created with the makeshift bedding. She tried all she could to drop back off to sleep but sleep never came. She had slept for so long already. Eventually the pressure became too much to bear, the dam was creaking. With another huff of agitation, she disentangled herself from the covers, got herself up, unlocked the door and headed out on to the landing. It was as dark as a sewer. Searching for a light switch she felt her way along, the rippled remnants of embossed wallpaper gently massaging her finger tips as she ran them along the wall. Eventually her fingers caught the wooden architrave around the toilet doorway. She eased the door inwards and fumbled in the darkness for the corded pull switch that she knew was dangling just inside. With an audible click that seemed amplified by the silence of the hour, the tiny cubicle was engulfed in a brilliant yellow light.

'Jesus!' Felicity squeaked, she felt her bladder relax and she almost wet herself. Panicked, she grabbed between her legs in an attempt to stop the flow and to cover her modesty. Wide-eyed in shock she stared at the tall youth stood in the doorway, his hands glued to his zipper. Like a bizarre showroom mannequin, he stood rooted to the spot, clearly having just had a wee in the dark. His heavy donkey jacket gave him a wide frame. Light shone out from the loo reflecting off the jacket's leatherette shoulder panel. He seemed as shocked to find Felicity on the landing, as she was to find him there. His head was topped with a dark beanie hat. He wore heavy army trousers and black work boots with toes that had worn through so that you could see the metal toe caps. A canvas army surplus rucksack was slung over his right shoulder. Zipper closed, he moved his hands and shoved them deep in to the front pockets of his jacket.

Felicity, realizing that she was flashing more than she would have liked, clutched desperately at the hem of the 'Siouxsie and the Banshees' t-shirt she had borrowed. The length barely covered her nether regions. She kicked herself mentally as she remembered the knickers that Mel had given her, folded and ready for the morning, on the cool window sill.

He tilted his head slightly, the light catching his face, which had the effect of highlighting his bright eyes. Felicity noticed. She studied his jawline, clean shaven, well defined and mature. His bottom lip was accented by a thin scar that sliced down on to his chin.

His clothing smelled but she did not find it offensive. Rather, It was a warm, strong smell; a lived-in workman-like smell. There was something honest about it. He lifted his chin towards her. 'Good band.' Then he turned away and headed down the stairs. Felicity listened to the clump of his heavy boots on the stair treads, an occasional squeak from the aged-timber breaking the rhythm. A cool morning draft wafted up the through the house as he opened the front door. She heard the door close.

Felicity felt like she had held her breath for minutes. Internal sparks ran up her spine making her shiver, producing an involuntary smile to light up her face. The hairs on her body tingled, which she allowed herself to appreciate for a moment, a moment before she felt a small dribble of wee escape.

X

When she returned to the room, Mel was rousing. As Felicity entered, she sat up and stretched, rubbing at her naked eyes. The girl swung around and off the mattress, sliding in to a pair of ethnic-print baggy bottoms. 'Mornin', Flick.' Her voice was cigarette-hoarse. Mel made her way out of the room, leaving Felicity alone.

Felicity looked out of the window, down in to the back garden. It was a jungle of bramble and long-forgotten foliage that had grown unchecked for some time. The house felt like sanctuary after the chaos of the previous day. The sleep had served her well and there was a strange comfort to the place, a relaxed and free atmosphere that she could feel but did not quite understand yet. She had no idea of the time but knew it was early. The sun was yet to rise fully and though condensation ran in rivulets down the inside of the windows she could tell that it was going to be a pleasant day.

'Here you go, daydream dolly.' Mel arrived bearing two steaming cups of tea and a plate of buttered toast. She placed the breakfast on the sill next to Felicity, sliding a piece off for herself and jamming it in to her mouth. Then she turned back in to the room and perched herself on a small stool, facing the mirror on her shelf. 'Listen, Flick, I've got to go to work this morning but I knock off at five.' Mel leaned in to the mirror, her hair held back out of the way by a band. Using a pad, she applied a pale foundation to her skin.

'Where do you work?' Felicity had sat herself close by to watch Mel's routine. Mel's well-practised dexterity pleased her to see. It was like watching an artist at work.

'A little chemist, It's only just up the road, a little walk.' Coal-black outline had been applied to her eyes. 'I only do weekdays. It's okay, gives me some extra spending. They have a weekend girl so I don't have to work Saturdays which is cool'

Mel had filled in the outline around her eyes. The effect was as stunning as when Felicity had seen her the day before. Mel quaffed her cup of tea and turned her attention to her lips, initially creating a thin black outline. 'Good thing about working there,' She clicked the lid back on and waved the lipstick liner at Felicity. 'I get good discount.'

'The amount you get through you could keep a factory in business!'

Mel laughed. 'You cheeky mare!' She slipped an earring through her lobe. A silver cobweb dangled from the loop. "You could do with a bit of sprucing up yourself!'

Mel set to work on her hair. She teased at strands, pulling them outwards and upwards. Felicity choked on the fug of hairspray she used to set the black candy floss of hair. Mel opened the window further to clear the air.

'I Saw a bloke on the landing this morning.' Felicity fiddled with the hem of the t-shirt.

'Oh yeah? Who was it?' Mel was using her fingers, adding the final touches to her coiffure, pulling and sculpting her locks in to a voluminous ebony cloud.

'How would I know?' Felicity wrinkled her nose. 'Looked like a builder. Had scar on his lip.' She pointed at where the boy's scar was on her own lip.

Mel recognised the description immediately. 'Quiet.' She confirmed. 'Did he say much?' She laughed at her little joke.

Felicity raised her eyebrows. 'He said these are a good band.' She looked down at the borrowed top.

Mel chuckled. 'He's got good taste!' She was getting dressed for work. Black it was. She chose a black boat collar top, black leggings and a shiny, black PVC skirt that came to just below her bum. 'He's one of the skinhead crew that knock around together. They're mostly alright. You'll see them around a lot.' She tugged on a pair of pointy-toe suede pixie boots, black of course. A silver studded strap ran across the foot and behind the ankle. 'Did I see a little twinkle, Flick?' She teased.

'What?' Felicity's cheeks flushed. 'We hardly met!'

'Well, you know what they say,' Mel slipped a tabard over her shoulders, the yellow polyester clashed wonderfully with her outfit. 'First appearances can be important.' She nodded her head at Felicity. 'And to be fair, he probably got a good look at your meat rack!'

Felicity covered her face with her hands in mock embarrassment.

'Anyway, enough small talk. I need to get going.' Mel grabbed her satchel. 'If you're gonna stick around we need to get you a job or signed on the dole. You're gonna need some cash.' Mel gave the room a cursory check before making a move. 'Make yourself at home.' Felicity heard the girl chuckling as she left.

******

It was Monday. Felicity had managed to work that out. It felt like an age ago she had done her moonlight flit from the home, so much had happened in that short period of time that it seemed impossible. Now, here she was in a strange house with a strange arrangement in a strange room in strange clothes among strange folk. But she liked it, it felt okay. Felicity went downstairs to the kitchen. Pans of water had been heated on the hob and the kettle was still warm. She took a pan up to the bathroom and filled the sink. She had borrowed some of Mel's toiletries so was able to give herself a good scrub and brush her teeth. She returned to the room feeling renewed and it was not only attributable to a stand-up flannel wash, thorough though it had been. She had an air of positivity about her, something she had not felt for some time. Despite the lack of permanence or security the current situation offered her, it was infinitely more preferable to the anxious uncertainty of her last few weeks in the home.

Mel had given her the go-ahead to borrow some clothes. Felicity ran her hands across the rack of clothing, a potpourri of different weaves, materials and textures tickled her fingertips. She perused the piles on the shelf. Unsurprisingly, colour options were limited but Felicity picked out a khaki vest top and skinny black jeans. The waist fit was adequate and though they were too long for her, being that Mel was quite a bit taller, she rolled the hems of the jeans up a couple of turns. Her feet were drying up well, the sores and blistered skin hardening. The bed rest had served her well. Satisfied with the inspection, she slipped on a pair of socks before turning her attention to the plethora of footwear lined up, military neat, beneath the rack. The pair of black Dr Marten boots that Mel had been wearing when they met took her fancy. There was a handy loop at the ankle that made it easier for her to pull them on. It was a relief to find that they fitted well. They were well broken in, the leather supple and malleable, very unlike the clumpy work boots she had arrived in. She wriggled her toes around and was pleased to find that they had no steel toe caps.

She sat and ran a big brush through her locks. She gritted her teeth as she pulled the bristles through tangles. It was a question of perseverance, her hair was not too dirty, she had showered only yesterday, but she had not had a chance to run a brush or comb through it for a long time. When she was happy, she cleaned her hair from the brush bristles, it was then that she noticed the small scabs of dried blood trapped in the bird's nest.

Felicity stood back from the mirror and held her breath, she was taken aback to see what she had become. To her, the transformation was incredible, a simple change of clothing had seen her emerge from an awkward and stunted teenager to an edgy and confident-looking young rebel. The jeans sat snug on her waist accentuating her hips. The vest had loose, low-cut armholes that showed her bra strap, it added something provocative to the outfit. She had a figure. Not a classic hourglass shape, she was slight, well-hipped and small boobed, but she could see that she had developed in to a young woman.

Independent expression and creativity had been carefully managed in the home. Staid, appropriate clothing and sensible footwear had been encouraged by the regime. A visiting mobile hairdresser had visited every few weeks, Felicity had never been asked how she would like it trimmed. She and some of the older girls had been well aware of the fashion trends that evolved in the outside world beyond the tall walls, they had seen girls at school who dared to make small statements to their uniform; a shortened skirt, a loosened tie or a button badge pinned to a blazer lapel. These were often short-lived adjustments, as once noticed by a teacher or snotty monitor, the offender would find themselves reprimanded and ordered to return their customized garb back to the norm. To not do so, risked being temporarily suspended from the school. Serious transgression could see a girl permanently removed.

Felicity's options had always been less than narrow. Where had she ever had the opportunity to purchase alternative clothing of her choice or a button badge that expressed her love for a pop band? Any off-site visits had been strictly chaperoned.

That was why the kids had loved their weekly allowance of 'Top of the Pops'. It was their portal to another world, a colourful and vibrant fantasy where young people could dress for fun, dance awkwardly to the latest pop hits and stumble in to the floor cameras that bullied a pathway through the audience.

She swung her head slightly; her shoulder length locks tickled her shoulders. Her hair would have to wait.

Felicity had been blessed, or cursed, depending on one's viewpoint, with ceaseless energy. It was another trait that she had little knowledge about, how she had inherited it, but it made it difficult to stay put. She spent some time sat on the mattress thumbing through a couple of amateur-printed booklets relating to some of the bands she had seen written on the cassette tapes the night before. They were fan publications, obviously aimed at like-minded youths. Type-written reviews of gigs, record releases, films and literature, humorous soundbites and observation pieces were scattered with poorly printed images of bands, people, characters, the pictures were really hard to make out, the printing format did not lend itself well to the replication of cut and paste.

She tossed the fanzine aside and decided she would have to amuse herself, she had time to kill.

She bolted the bedroom door and made her way through the house. The landing was dark, all the other bedroom doors were closed. The only natural light crept up the stairs from the hallway below, barely making any impact. She chose to head further up through the house. The staircase to the upper level was much narrower, an add-on, an extension leading to the what had once been loft space. Every stair tread groaned under her meagre weight. Even at this level, the plaster had hemorrhaged stretching the garish wallpaper to the point of splitting. A large area had popped open like a gunshot wound, the plaster had long ago fallen and been cleared. She came to a tiny landing. Yet even that small space had two doors that led off it. She pushed gently against a thickly painted door, a biohazard warning sign, bright yellow, showed humour. It held firm; she could hear no movement, its occupier obviously asleep or out for the day. She eased the other door and found a tiny washroom, no bath, just a toilet and sink. Whoever used it had painted the walls in a deep purple, a purple so dark that it was almost black. The boards were bare, displaying years of well-earned patina. A quick scan told her it was a double occupancy. Two toothbrushes, boy and girl toiletries. The smell was spicy and heady, earthy.

Her curiosity sated she head back down the stairs, past Mel's landing, down to the entrance hall. She had already seen the kitchen area so chose to explore elsewhere. She pushed open a door just off the entrance hallway. It opened in to a lounge area. A hotchpotch of recycled furnishings was dotted around the room. Floorboards ran the length of the room; a threadbare rug in the middle of the room was held in place by a rectangular coffee table. Last nights' dog-ends stagnated in an ashtray. A tiny scattering of tobacco and other unidentifiable debris, organic and sweet smelling, evidenced some industry. King-size rizla papers and torn pieces of card alongside the raw materials had been left messy on the surface. Felicity picked up a packet of cigarette papers and pulled one free. She screwed the paper in to a tight ball and rolled it between her fingers. She wandered around the room reading the walls. They were busy; contemporary film posters, band posters and protest movement posters covered the gaudy décor from the house's earlier period. Flyers aplenty demanded action, advertised gigs and invited attendance. Small pieces of graffiti, artistic and satirical were tolerated.

She left the room and ventured on, past another locked door adjacent to the lounge and the kitchen that led to the rear of the house. A narrow-paneled door under the main stairs seemed mysterious. She thumbed the latch and it gave, allowing her to ease it open. It was the entrance to the basement area of the house. She peered down in to the pitch black. No matter how hard she blinked she could not see down in to the space below. The dense blackness seemed impenetrable. She fumbled for a switch, her hands running over the coarse brickwork. The stairs looked unsafe, wonky and rickety. She dared not venture further without light. Her fingers found the switch. She turned the lights on.

'What the fuck!' An angry bellow, threatening in its intensity, tore up the stairs as the hazy yellow light diluted the blackness. Felicity almost died. So startled was she that she almost fell down the stairs. As she regained her balance, an enormous black combat boot hurtled up towards her with dangerous velocity. The boot nicked her ear and thumped in to the wall behind her. Suitably alerted, Felicity backed out as quick as she could. She did not hang around. She fled back to Mel's room where she slammed the door behind, locking herself in in the process. After a few incredibly anxious minutes, she was relieved to hear no pursuit. She squeezed her ear to the door to be absolutely sure. All was deathly silent. Not a creak, groan or murmur.

Satisfied that she was not about to be murdered by a madman, she unbolted the door and left the room again. She crept down the stairs, leaning over the banister rail she could see that the basement door was shut tight again. She let herself out of the front door and in to the glare of the morning sunshine. It was sunny in North London and the streets were alive, vehicles travelled noisily along both sides of the road. Both pavements were busy with pedestrians. Felicity had never seen so many different shades of skin colour.

Back in the home, two of the children had been of mixed heritage, a brother and sister, their mother had been white, their father a black man. She remembered that some of the staff and children had not been kind to them. 'Half-caste' was how she had heard them described.

Now she was out in the world. Not a microcosm of some little England that she had experienced growing up. She had known that there was a world outside the children's home, outside of her school life and the area that surrounded both establishments but she had not had the opportunity to experience it. She had not had time to stop and appreciate much in the last day or so either. Survival had been her priority so far.

The many shades, the assorted spice of accents and languages, the human soup of culture and costume fascinated her. She passed a pair of African women deep in conversation. The interaction was loud and animated, the cadence of their speech fast, almost like the stutter of a machine gun. The fabric of their clothing radiated warmth, so vibrant that it was hard to believe that you could make clothing that colourful. White folk bustled by; she heard the familiar accents of London. Noticed the tattoos on some of the men's hairy forearms, smelled the waft of setting lotion on some of the women's permed hair, saw the patched knees of the kid's jeans. All ages mingled and passed each other, calling out familiar greetings to those they recognised.

'Mornin' Renee.'

'How's your Ronnie?'

'See you at the club on Saturday.'

'Off to the doctors, me sinuses are playing havoc.'

A group of elderly gentlemen were sat talking blues. They were waiting for the local pub to open. A trilby-topped West Indian man slapped his thigh heavily as he told the punchline to a story. His acquaintances rocked on the low fence as they joined his merriment. The men spoke with strong accents; patois.

She came across an Asian man. He was sweeping the pavement down. He moved a triangular bin, the metal feet scraping on the paving, to sweep beneath it. He was muttering away under his shiny, black moustache. A woman in traditional Asian dress stood in the newsagent doorway. Her arms were folded and she seemed exasperated. A fold of her sari breezed from her head. Her hair was beautiful, deep black and shiny. A red dot marked her brow. The woman repositioned the bright silky covering. She spoke out animatedly towards the man. She spoke in her native tongue, Hindi.

Felicity stopped to observe their exchange. The man looked pained at the interjection from his wife. He ceased sweeping, her outburst had got his attention. He held out a hand in question. 'What can I do?' He gestured towards the shop. 'Who else can I ask to manage shop? I cannot do everything myself. All I ask is that you serve the counter while I stock shelves, clean, take delivery and do orders.' His wife responded in Hindi. It fascinated Felicity to hear the interaction carried out in dual language.

'Of course, I know that!' He was frustrated. 'They are late again. I cannot give the sack if they not here! I don't know if they will turn up to today. I rely on these people. I need someone to mind the shop. Who else can I call on?'

'I could do it.' Speaking her mind was becoming a habit. Felicity stood and smiled as the man took in her appearance. He looked back at his wife and their agitated interaction continued.

'I wouldn't be late.' She spoke out louder, more assertively, without being rude. Her persistence caught their attention.

'What? You want a job?' The man did not seem to take her seriously.

'Yeah, I wouldn't have butted in if I didn't, would I?'

The man absorbed her comment. He looked at his wife then back at Felicity. 'You have worked in shop before?' It was a fair question.

'No, but everyone's got to start somewhere, right?' It was a fair response.

The man spoke to his wife in Hindi. She shrugged, gave a dismissive gesture with her hand and turned away heading back in to the shop. 'Okay, trial period.' He looked at her for some acknowledgement. 'Thirty-pound a week.'

'Sounds good. When can I start?'

XI

It had been a good start. Mr Chowdury had been keen to get her started on the shop floor and once given a run through, she had soon got the hang of stocking the shelves. He had busied himself behind the counter and checking in deliveries, leaving her to her chores. She had felt important, something that did not come naturally to her. It was satisfying to be given charge of something, even if it was only a three-foot aisle and boxes of baked beans. What really gave her a lift was to be awarded trust. She was nervous when Mr Chowdury had asked her to mind the till for a bit. He had an important call to make. He gave her a quick till lesson then disappeared to the rear of the shop. Felicity wondered if it was a test, to see how trustworthy she could be. She was determined to show him that she was. She had never seen so much currency in one place. When he had given her the initial coaching on working the till and the cash draw had shot open with a clatter, she had fought to hide her amazement at the orderly trays padded with notes and coins, each tray holding a particular denomination. Mr Chowdury had explained the idea of a float, the funds that needed to be there in order to provide change for customers purchases, and that at the close of business each day he 'cashed up' to check what the earnings had been made that day.

She soon noticed that there were peak periods, she had already missed the early mixed rush of commuter patronage and local regulars who stopped in for their daily rags and ciggies but lunchtime had tested her and she reckoned she had coped well considering how new she was to the grind. A couple of punters had enquired after her, surprised to see a new face in the shop. She had appreciated the interest and enjoyed chatting with a couple of the elderly customers.

During the quiet times she had familiarized herself with the stock. A kaleidoscopic array of brands and produce. Her backdrop was a wall of cigarette packets, cigars, tobacco pouches, cigarette papers, lighters and matchboxes. A calendar, exotic and bright with reds, oranges and yellows was hung from the racking. At the head of the calendar was a mystical image of a bejeweled elephant-like creature upon an ornate throne. The bold script was a linguistic tangle of two languages, English and Hindi. The tobacconist section seemed the most popular port of call for the steady train of customers. She had quickly become familiar with where the most commonly bought brands sat and could locate them quickly. Mr Chowdury had been suitably impressed.

She had a spring in her step as she headed back to the house. The sun had warmed the road, sweating tarmac and dusty concrete replaced the spice of incense in her nostrils. The thin pungent smoke from the smoldering sticks had drifted from the rear in to the main shop throughout the day. It was a powerful and heady scent that had taken some getting used to but after a couple of hours she hardly noticed it. She supped at a can of sticky sweet Tizer with some satisfaction. The tin was moist and cool. A gift from Mr Chowdury, he had refused to take it off her wages, he was that pleased with her efforts.

It was not long before she approached the house. The wall that bordered the front garden was crazed; lumps of render had broken loose exposing the brick work beneath. The white wash was streaked, green and grey, like a cheap marble, stained by road traffic pollution. Arriving at the front gate Felicity froze. A gaggle of youths were congregated in the front yard. Two lads kicked a football to each other, a game of keepy-ups. Good natured banter was heard when either of them failed to keep the ball off the floor. They reminded her of the two boys Mel had spoken with in Carnaby Street the previous day. They were not the same boys but one of them was wearing a similar top in bright white honeycomb cotton, collared with contrasting blue tips and the same embroidered laurel wreath on the chest. The other was sweating through a white crew neck t-shirt, a custom-printed motif on the front declared 'Hackney skins'. The boy's head was oddly-shaped, slightly elongated, almost oval; nut-like. A couple, a girl and a boy, squatted on the steps that led up to the entrance. They were loosely entwined, his arm draped across her shoulders, she, tucked in to his side. The boy's jeans were tight, his legs splayed, the denim crotch threatened his chances of fatherhood. A fresh, pastel-yellow button-down shirt matched the sunshine. Navy blue braces crossed his shoulders adding contrast. His girl, tucked under his wing, watched the horseplay below them with mild amusement. Her Bleached blonde hair stood firm and punky. An 'Anti-Nowhere league' emblazoned cap-sleeve tee topped a short skirt and fishnet-tight clad bottom. A cassette player was perched on the step just behind them.

The sound was mono, vintage sounding, and yet, perfectly fitting for the summer day and the relaxed gathering.

I said stick it up mister
Hear what I say, sir

Get your hands in the air, sir
And you will get no hurt mister
Do what I say sir
Just what I mean sir
Get your hands in the air, sir
And you will get no hurt, no

Felicity did recognize the skinhead stood under the porch in the shade. It was the same boisterous lad that she and Mel had passed in the hallway at teatime the evening before. Ronnie was still topless, his braces continued to play no part in keeping his jeans up. The jeans he wore had been customized, areas had been bleached white, marbling the blue denim. He wore ankle length boots, blood-rich in colour with airwair soles. Stretched out along a low white concrete balustrade lounged the skinhead from her brief encounter earlier that morning. He had not changed out of his work clothes, though he had ditched his heavy donkey jacket. He cradled a large brown bottle of cider in his hands.

Quiet.

In among all the festivities, it was the stunning appearance of the girl that stood in the doorway leaning against the door jamb that held Felicity's attention. It was not without some competition for her attention, being that Quiet was close by but the girl won through. The girl's appearance was shocking.

Shocking, yes, but shockingly beautiful.

I said yeah (I said yeah), listen what I say (listen what I say)
I said hear me now, (yeah, yeah) listen what I say

It was a look that some would call daring, some would call anarchic, and some would call provocative. Felicity had never seen a hair style like it. She was used to seeing boys with cropped heads, there were five in the front yard at that moment. Crops of different graded length with subtle touches. The boy with the girl on the steps had grown sideburns, his hair dark, they were neat and shaped to compliment his cut. One of the football players had an ultra-thin parting cut in to the crown of his number two crop.

But this was a game changer as far as Felicity was concerned.

Fifty-four forty-six, that's my number

Raven-haired, her dome was shorn short, not bald but much, much shorter than the length that had been deliberately left to accentuate the style. The longer locks had been carefully left to add contrast against the cropped crown, flowing from the rear of her scalp down covering her neck to tickle her shoulders. Other pieces snaked around her ears and a shorter length kissed her forehead.

Felicity had seen punk hairstyles. They were wild and colourful, they were designed to attract attention and to cause people to stare in shock or wonderment but the girl's hair cut seemed different. It was both subtle and unsubtle at the same time. The way it was carried, almost utilitarian in design, similar to the boy's cut but clearly feminine. A statement, that much was clear, but rather than a statement to others it felt more personal, more a statement to the girl's sense of self. It was powerful.

Felicity had become so fixated on the details of the hair style that she was unaware of the length of time she stood gawping. The fresh aroma of sun-warmed foliage erupted around her as the football bundled in to the privet next to her. She blinked.

'What the fuck you staring at?'

Stick it up, mister, hear what I say, sir, yeah
Get your hands in the air, sir
And you will get no hurt, mister, oh oh
Stick it up, mister, hear what I say, sir, yeah

The girl had moved from the doorway and was stood on the top step. The two lovers had heard the challenge and had turned to look up at the girl's clearly agitated inquiry.

The one-a-side football match had been postponed. The star players stayed on the pitch, the importance of retrieving the ball had been shelved by their diverted interest in the girl's verbal challenge for the moment.

Formidable and threatening, the girl glared down at Felicity awaiting some response.

Yet, Felicity could not look away.

Street tough, the girl's choice of fashion was unyielding and yet there was an edgy, sensual effect to her outfit that was hard to describe.

There was a masculinity to the shirt she wore, tartan-checked in blues and yellows, a bias-cut placket buttoned up to an open neck. The girl had left the top button undone. This allowed the button-down collars of the shirt to sit away from her neck where a small silver chain could be seen. The shirt was short-sleeved. The cut of the garment was darted. This alone served to compliment her waist but the fit across her chest and shoulders created a silhouette that was simply stunning, the cloth and shape of the shirt oozed class.

The shirt hem was tucked in to a pair of straight-legged jeans. These were well fitted again but not super tight and finished off at the bottom with a reverse turn up, a hem of around an inch. A gap between the hem of the jeans and the girl's shoes showed off bright red terry toweling socks. Her choice of footwear, again, suggested masculinity. They were slip-ons, heavy black leather loafers. Round-toed with a moc-front. A pair off tassels dangled from the shoe's apron.

Her pale arms were held by her side, fists clenched.

Felicity ventured to the bottom of the steps. The girl met her at the bottom step. This gave her a considerable height advantage over Felicity. She looked menacing and ready for conflict.

'I said, what the fuck are you lookin' at?'

'You look great.' And she meant it.

'What?' The girl screwed her nose up in confusion and gave a snort. 'You takin' the piss?'

'Not at all.' Felicity continued. 'You look stunning.'

'Fuckin' hell!' The girl was incredulous. She shook her head lightly. 'You are either very bent, very stupid or very brave.'

'Bent?' Felicity had never heard the expression.

'Yes, bent, gay, lezzy!' The girl looked behind checking for some sense of coherence from her friends.

Felicity laughed at the words. They reminded her of the faux-pas she had made with Mel the previous evening.

Triggered by what she deduced was Felicity making fun of her, the girl exploded. 'Very stupid, it is then!'

She grabbed at Felicity's vest and drew back her fist.

'Woah!' A male voice interjected, calling a halt to the proceedings. Felicity breathed out. Ronnie had caught the girl's cocked arm. Felicity was thankful but felt he had left it a little late!

'She's Mel's mate.' He blurted. Initially amused, he had let the scenario run on a bit but could see that things were coming to a head. He had stepped in at the right moment. 'It's cool, she stayed with Mel last night.' His interruption was the perfect extinguisher, fire quenched, Ronnie relaxed his grip on the girl's arm.

'That don't explain why she was staring at me. I don't like people staring at me.'

Felicity spoke. 'I meant it. I love your hair.' She offered explanation. 'I'm not gay or stupid or brave. Just like what you're wearing, that's all. Where did you get it done?'

The girl shrugged off friendly skinhead's hand. 'Alright, Ronnie. You can back off now.'

'You know, you're a bit fuckin' weird.' The girl observed.

Felicity chuckled. 'You don't know the half of it! What's your name?'

The girl softened. 'Jan. It's Janice but I prefer Jan.'

'Felicity, Mel calls me Flick. I like that.'

Satisfied that all was settled, Ronnie introduced himself properly to Felicity. Gavin and Shirley nodded their acquaintance, they seemed friendly enough. The two budding football superstars were introduced, each performing a theatrical bow for her, Micky in the polo top and, Hackney skin with the odd-shaped head was Peanut. There was no need to ask why. Jan sat on the bottom step where Felicity joined her. The sun had warmed the concrete up and the heat was pleasant, radiating through the black denim of her jeans in to her buttocks.

'Where you from?' Jan pulled a packet of ten cigarettes from her breast pocket. Sticking the fag between her lips she offered Felicity the packet. She shook her head politely. 'Gis a light.' Jan reached behind her to take a box of matches from Gavin. 'Seriously, where you from, Flick?' Jan took along drag.

'Essex. But I'm going to live here now.' Felicity was hedging her bets. She had no idea if Mel would put her up for more nights but it was a bridge that would need crossing sooner rather than later.

'I live with my mum and dad down the road. Stoke Newington way. Do you know it?'

Felicity shook her head. 'Do you come here a lot?'

'Mostly. I knock around with these divs don't I!' Jan said it loud enough for all to hear. Ronnie stuck his middle finger up in her direction.

Felicity could tell that the group were good friends. There was a relaxed air to the way they spent their time together. Humorous quips and observations were exchanged and they moved freely around each other. Quiet was, well, quiet but he was involved. He tapped his boot to the rhythm of the reggae music being played on the cassette player. He regularly offered swigs of his cider to the others. When it was passed her way, Felicity caught the scent of the strong appley refreshment in her nostrils, it was invigorating and pleasant. She took a mouthful and liked it. Wiping the bottle top with her hands she handed it to Micky.

'I was serious, you know. I love your hair. Where did you get it cut?'

'Mate does it.' Jan spoke as if having your hair cut by a friend was an every-day event.

'I'd like my hair like that.'

'Really?' Jan studied Felicity's clothing. 'You don't look much like a skinhead to me?'

'Well, who knows? Maybe I want to be a skinhead!'

Jan laughed. 'We can sort it if you're serious? I've done a couple of feather cuts before. All we need is clippers.'

Jan leaned back; she spoke directly to Ronnie. 'Have you got your clippers handy?'

******

They set up in the lounge, Felicity perched on an old upturned plastic beer crate. They had found a towel and draped it around her shoulders. Jan weighed Felicity's hair in her hands. 'You sure about this, Flick?' Jan gave the handful of hair a squeeze. 'Once we start there's no going back!'

Felicity was resolute. As soon as she had spotted Jan in the doorway earlier, she had desired to have her hair cut in the same style. 'I'm positive. You do know what you're doing though?'

'Yeah, like I said, we all give each other a trim up now and again. I've done this for a couple of other mates.' The thrum of the clippers started up as Jan threw the switch. 'Don't bloody move!'

Jan took her time, careful, measuring and checking constantly throughout the cut. Felicity tingled with Jan's touch; she had not received this much attention for a long time. She enjoyed the sensation of the clippers vibrating close to her scalp. Clumps of her blonde locks fell away, piece by piece until her lap was carpeted with hair. Jan concentrated on trimming and shaping her fringe. 'You know, you've got lovely eyes, Flick.' It was a nice observation. Felicity had rarely experienced personal compliments, especially about her appearance. She played with a few strands between her fingers, concentrating on keeping still. She could now feel Jan's breath on her crown as her hair thinned out further.

'Do you want me to leave the length at the back, Flick' Jan had stopped to cast her eye over her work.

'I like yours, long at the back.'

'Okay, I'll leave the length. You can always take it down shorter if you want later.' She laughed. 'Can't stick it back on, can we!'

Felicity was impressed by Jan's attention to detail and her deft touch as she applied the finishing touches. She felt sure that Jan was doing a good job. Finally, Jan straightened and flicked the clippers off. 'Well, I reckon the job's a good'un.' She ran her hands over Felicity's dome, flicking shards of hair away with her finger tips. Felicity erupted in goose bumps, Jan's touch tingling her newly shorn cranium.

'Go on. Have a butchers,' Jan encouraged her. 'See what you think. I think it looks great personally.'

Felicity approached a mirror stood on the mantlepiece. She had no idea what to expect, no preconceived image in her head of what she would look like. She only had Jan's own feather cut to compare it to. Jan's cut looked amazing but their hair was very different. Jan's hair was almost jet-black with a lot of weight to it. Felicity's own hair was blonde, light and wispy.

She held her breath as she stepped to the mirror.

When she saw herself, her mouth dropped wide open. The transformation was astounding. The fringe, sides and tail almost floated around the graduated crop.

Jan noticed her pleasure. She let out a breath of relief. She teased at the tail of Felicity's new haircut. 'Your hair is lovely. Really suits the cut.'

Jan wrapped the lead around the clippers.

'It looks like real feathers.'

******

With trepidation, Felicity stepped out on to the porch. She loved her new cut but was unsure what the others would make of it.

A wolf whistle shrilled. Micky had stopped to take in the view and was impressed. Removing his fingers from his lips he nodded hard in appreciation. Peanut stopped the ball at his feet and had a good gander. 'Wow! It really suits you!' Shirley the punk was in agreement. Gav nodded his support. Ronnie flapped like a land-stranded carp, his mouth opening and shutting while he stood up, sat down then stood up again.

'Cheers.' She was really appreciative of the gang's approval but what she really sought was the approval of a particular person. She summoned up the courage and let her eyes wander to her right and got her reward. Quiet lifted himself up to a sitting position, his heavy boots swinging, the heels bouncing against the concrete.

'Proper feathers.' He said quietly. 'Suits them blue eyes.'

XII

'You don't do anything by halves do you!' Mel sat cross-legged on the mattress, forking rice and beans in to her mouth. She gestured with the fork. 'Less than twenty-four hours and you've upset our resident troll in the basement, ventured in to the depths of Hackney, won yourself a job, almost got yourself a pasting from Jan's jackhammer, made up with Jan and made friends with the kids from Clockwork Orange and,' She paused swallowing a mouthful of food. 'Got yourself a jolly spiffin' new hairdo, even if I say so myself!' She laughed sending flecks of rice across the room.

Felicity poked at her bowl of food. When it was said like that, it seemed impossible. Without a doubt the last few days had been the most terrifying and exhilarating days in her life, in equal measures.

Meeting Mel had been the huge piece of luck she had needed. When she had shinned down the drainpipe at the home, she had dared not dream of being where she was sat right then. Mel was right, things had been eventful but she was safe for now, she had access to shelter, food, she had funds available to her on Friday and she had made some friends.

Friends. Felicity had friends at the home but it was not the same. She had never enjoyed the opportunity to have any real social life or to meet other young people outside the home. She spoke to some of the girls at school but always chose to keep her distance. They treated her differently, not badly but different to the others who were not looked-after kids. She had never been invited to their homes for tea or to their birthday parties.

'Let me rub your head!' Mel leaned forward and run her palm across Felicity's scalp. 'Feels so cool! Does it feel weird? I mean, you've never had your hair as short as this before, have you?'

'It feels nice. I wanted it to be like Jans.' Felicity fiddled with one of her side locks. She spooned some food in to her mouth but for some reason did not feel very hungry. 'I want to be a skinhead.'

'Fair enough, they're a good bunch,' Mel paused. 'Mostly.' She put her empty bowl to one side. 'You've got a bit of spending money now so you can buy yourself some gear.'

'That's what I need to talk to you about, Mel.' Felicity put her bowl on top of the other. 'This is your room and I can't stay in here forever. You'll soon get fed up with sharing your space. Me? I'm used to it. I shared a dorm with other girls but it's not fair on you.' Felicity let Mel digest what she had said before continuing, 'Now I've got some work I could pay a little bit. I just need to find somewhere reasonable that's all.'

Mel was thinking. That done, she patted Felicity on the knee. 'Leave it with me, Flick.' She jumped up. 'I've got an idea, no promises but it might work out.' She rattled through the cassette cases. 'But for now, let's have some music.'

******

They were both up bright and early, Mel going through her usual routine as she got ready for work. Felicity followed in her wake, borrowing another top and promising to get the previous day's garment loan cleaned. Mel dismissed her. 'Chuck it on the pile.' She pointed to a jumble of black in the corner of the room. She was concentrating on her eye make-up. 'I've got to do a laundry run soon anyway.' Felicity added the vest and underwear to the pile. She watched as Mel carried out the meticulous process, the outline first then the in-fill. Tilting her head, she checked for symmetry. Satisfied, she turned away from the mirror.

'You look like Cleopatra.' Felicity remembered the artists impression of the Egyptian Queen she had seen in history books.

'Now, that's a compliment!' Mel chirped. 'Thanks.'

'Could you do mine?'

'Yeah, why not.' Mel offered her the seat. 'Plonk yourself down here and we'll see what we can do.'

Mel got started. 'I think we need to be a bit more subtle. Not sure you'd suit a Siouxie special, not with your new feather cut.' Felicity held still, allowing Mel to weave her magic. The application tickled at times; she had never worn make-up.

'There you go. See what you think.' Mel held the mirror for her.

Her eyes had been lined in black adding small cat-like points at the corners. The effect drew the sparkling blue of her eyes out. 'I love it! Thanks, Mel.'

Mel gave her the gee up. 'Come on, can't afford to be late.'

******

It was a shock. Mr. Chowdury was polite but she could see that he did not know what to make of the transformation to her appearance. She had not given it a second thought and had waltzed in to the store, chirpy and ready for her second day at the grindstone. 'Morning!' Her energetic greeting startled him, he closed the glass front to the chilled cabinet and when he turned to acknowledge her, his eyes widened. He made no comment to her appearance, erring on the side of diplomacy, only offereing a good morning before setting her up with some tasks. He probably hoped that these new cosmetic alterations would not affect her work ethic.

The early papers had already gone out, the old boys were early risers and liked to get their tabloids before breakfast, but a steady flow of customers ensured that she was kept occupied. The small talk and gossip amused her. Folk chatted away oblivious to whoever was in earshot. Opinions were given and the gospel was read. Through this she acquired some understanding of the workings and etiquette that made up the local North London community. Names and habits started to become familiar.

During her lunchbreak she found a spot out front where she sat and tucked in to a packet of salt and vinegar crisps. She enjoyed 'people watching'. It was a privilege she had never been allowed before. All shapes, ages, colours and cultures passed as she sat there. Most paid her no mind but occasionally, she received a nod or a stare. The men tended to be nodders, the women the starers.

Mrs. Chowdury appeared in the shop doorway. She looked over to Felicity who smiled at her, the gesture was not returned. Mrs. Chowdury seemed to maintain an appearance of severity. The woman shuffled over to the low fencing and perched herself there, she sat a small distance from Felicity and seemed to be making an effort not to engage with her. It was a very visible aloofness. Felicity wondered if the woman was happy.

Her outfit was intricately patterned with bright swirling colour. It was a more casual outfit than the traditional sari, the overshirt known as a salwar and the loose-fitting trousers kameez. A pair of cheap rubber flip-flops protected the soles of her feet from any potential encounters with broken glass or dog shit. 'What have you done?'

Felicity looked round at the woman. It was hard to ascertain the woman's intent. Was it a scold?

'What do you mean?' Felicity asked.

'Your hair!' The woman gesticulated; her hand held out like an accusatory blade. 'Your lovely hair! Why did you cut it off?'

Felicity squirmed. How should she respond? It was clear to her that the woman was not being nasty, her tone seemed to be one of concern rather than rebuke. How could she explain her reasoning to this lady? Their cultures were oceans apart, literally; in philosophy, in values, in understanding.

'Why have you got your nose pierced?'

Mrs. Chowdury touched the stud that pierced her nostril. It was as if Felicity had reminded her that it was there. Circular in shape, it was made of a brighter, yellower gold than Felicity had seen before.

'My nath?' She turned slightly so that she and Felicity could see each other. 'This is a symbol of my maturity. Something that Hindu girls can have when they become young woman. They are now ready for marriage.' She looked to Felicity for confirmation of her understanding. 'This is how I show my respect for the Hindu goddess Parvati.'

'That is fascinating.' And she meant it. It was not a patronization. Felicity was curious, a raw sponge ready to absorb life experiences and knowledge. She took the opportunity to engage with the woman. 'I suppose in some weird way, Mrs. Chowdury, my haircut is a symbol of my own maturity. People have always told me how I should have my hair cut or what clothes I should wear. Now, I get to make those choices for myself. Do you know what I mean?'

She allowed the woman to absorb what she had said before continuing. 'You have your beliefs, your religion. My choice to have my hair cut like this or to dress a certain way makes me feel better, I get to hang around with a group of people that I enjoy being around.'

Mrs. Chowdury rocked her head side to side in a form of acknowledgement. 'You are a young woman who knows her mind.' She stood, pressing her hands in to her lower back and leaned backwards, letting out a small groan.

Felicity scrunched the empty crisp bag in to a ball and followed the shuffling woman back to work, she dropped the litter in to the bin outside the shop front.

As they reached the entrance, Mrs. Chowdury stopped suddenly, Felicity almost ran in to the back of her. The woman was short and it was a stretch but she reached up uninvited, and ran the palm of her hand over the fuzz of Felicity's haircut. She gave a shiver and chuckled. She pointed to Felicity's face.

'Your eyes? Your eyes I like. Pretty girl.'

******

Mel was out for the night with a boyfriend. She warned Felicity that she may not be back until late, if at all, that night. She gave a cheeky wink as she left. 'I'll try not to turn in to a pumpkin!'

Felicity had put a tin of beans on the hob and some bread in the toaster. The house was quiet, she daydreamed, gazing out the rear window. Life was pretty good at that moment. The beans bubbled, she turned to reduce the heat.

'Hello Feathers.'

Quiet had crept upon her again; he was making a habit of startling her but she was happy that he had. At least her nether regions were well covered this time!

He smiled, 'Sorry, didn't mean to make you jump.' He leaned across and turned the heat down for her.

'You didn't!' Felicity felt silly.

'What you cooking?' It was small talk.

'Beans,' It was obvious, 'on toast.' The toast popped up. They met awkwardly, squeezing past each other, her towards the toaster and he towards the sink. Felicity coloured up instantly, her cheeks flushed with red. He noticed and it tickled him but he was sensitive enough not to mention it. He liked it, she was cute, a little pocket rocket that was for sure. He dropped his plate and cutlery in to the sink and poured some water from the kettle over the dishes. He busied himself cleaning them while she flustered and flapped over plating up her meal. She turned to find him offering a knife and fork, still warm from the water but spotless. She took them. She felt slight resistance, as if he was holding them for a little too long, enjoying the moment of contact.

'Thanks.'

'Where you eating?' He was looking down at his hands as he dried them on a tea towel. It was an attempt not to unnerve her. He was a lot taller than her.

'Was going back up to Mel's room.' She rebalanced the plate of beans as they threatened to spill over. 'Why?' It was brave of her, she wanted him to elaborate, to keep the conversation going.

'No reason,' It was an attempt to appear non-plussed but he could not contain himself, 'was just going to suggest I keep you company if you were going to the lounge. But no big deal, just fancied a chat.'

She smiled, 'You know what? That sounds like a better plan.'

*****

The lounge was empty. She ate some of the food but her appetite was not great which was not a problem as the remainder was polished off by Quiet, whose real name, he informed her, happened to be Jim. 'Ronnie's brain wave.' He elaborated. 'He's usually the one that makes up nicknames for people. People always asking why I'm so quiet, I suppose it had to happen. I don't really mind. Keeps idiots away from me!' he paused and gave a short snigger. 'Better than being called peanut, I suppose.'

She was more interested in his appetite. He had already eaten after finishing work, a portion of pie and mash bought on the way home, washed down with a smothering of liquor and a can of Merrydown cider and yet, he had not missed a beat in clearing the remnants of her own plate. 'Always eat well, me. Working with my hands is what does it.' He held his hands out for her to see the callouses on his palms. His hands were the size of shovels. 'All that physical work burns it off.' He patted his stomach. 'No major issues yet!'

They talked for a long time. He was easy to sit with, very relaxed. He told her about the house. It was rented from an organization at a good price. The houses in the row had been condemned some years back, earmarked for demolition in the future. He explained that they were of Victorian construction, built in the 1900s and that they were now suffering from serious concrete fatigue and other structural issues that were uneconomical to repair. They would demolish the row in time and build new housing in the area.

She was surprised when he informed her that basement troll was the main player. He decided who came and went. He was considerably older, very private and did not mix with the other occupants. Quiet told her that the man worked nightshifts which explained his upset over her intrusion.

She knew all about Mel. Ronnie had the back room behind the lounge. Ronnie and Quiet had been friends since primary school, brought up on the same council estate. Their mums were good friends too. Ronnie worked as a tyre fitter. Felicity thought it an odd job for someone to do, fitting tyres to people's cars all day.

Jethro and Fern were interesting. She had yet to meet them. 'Anarchist-hippy dippies.' Was how Quiet had described them. They were an older and politically active pair by all accounts. He told her of the couple's belief in the abolition of all government and that they believed society should be encouraged to cooperate on a voluntary basis without threat of government interference or force. Felicity understood the flyers stuck on the lounge wall a bit better. 'They like a bit of mumbo-jumbo stuff as well, in to all this Dalai Lama meditation stuff. You can hear them chanting away sometimes.' He chuckled. 'Fuck knows what they're saying!' He paused, 'Love their grass too! Open their door and it's like happy valley, takes ages to clear!' He mimed smoking a reefer and being under influence. 'Whatever floats your boat, I suppose.'

Parts of the house's community, its rich tapestry of life were slotting in to place, the different scraps of human story being threaded together by Quiet's candid observations on his housemates. She remembered the somewhat sickly-sweet smog that often crept on to the landing from the master bedroom. Her lack of worldly experience meant that she had assumed that the aroma was attributable to some exotic cooking or potion brewing but she was learning stuff all the time. This was the closest she had ever been to illegal drugs as far as she was aware.

'Up top, you've got froggy.'

'Froggy?' She checked. Was this another nickname?

'Alexis, he's a French bloke, we don't really call him froggy, that's just me taking the piss. He's over here studying at uni or something. He's a good bloke, friendly enough, likes his punk, got good taste. His bird stays over sometimes.'

Quiet, Jim, was just eighteen. He had been a labourer since leaving school just before his sixteenth birthday. He was getting the skills and hoped to specialize sooner or later. It was a kind of apprenticeship, you learned as you went. He was lucky, he told her, he was treated well unlike some labourers he knew. He fancied himself as a brickie, a brick layer, in the future.

The time passed, she felt comfortable in his company and she knew that she was attracted to him. The butterflies doing aerobatics in her belly told her that! Though she was unfamiliar with the dance of romance, those little nuances, instinct, told her that her feelings were reciprocated. He was funny and open, chatting as if they had known each other for years. She did not have much to say herself but he had listened when she had. She told him about life at the home, that she did not know who her parents were, about things she liked; history and London. But she was careful, she held on to details about her life that even she had difficulty excepting. No point in scaring the poor bloke off!

They both had work in the morning. 'Listen, don't take this the wrong way but I've enjoyed tonight.' He was signing off. 'How do you feel about going out with me on Saturday? You know, let me show you some sights?' Felicity was taken aback by his invitation. Her cheeks flared again; being fair-haired and light-skinned, it annoyed her that she could not control it. She wondered how she could take his request the wrong way. It was an odd comment. She tried not to overthink it. Quiet sat expectantly.

'I'd like that.' She finally squeaked.

'That's sorted then.' He got up from the sofa. 'Better hit the sack got a lot of block work to move around tomorrow.'

Felicity followed his lead. As they approached the door, they came close together. It was an accident, just a matter of trajectory but sparks flew. He gently gripped her forearm encouraging her to turn. As she turned, she was level with his chest. Freshly bathed, he smelled strongly of soap. His other hand lifted her chin so that she looked up in to his face. The thin, pale scar that slashed from his lip into the cleft of his chin only made him more attractive. With his fingertips he tucked a lock of her hair behind her ear and ran his palm over her cropped scalp down to the nape of her neck. The long tails of hair entwined in his fingers. She could feel the roughness of his hands as they caressed her skin. She liked it a lot.

'You know, you've got gorgeous eyes, Feathers.'

He kissed her and she let him.

It was Felicity that broke away first. It was not that she was unhappy, quite the opposite. She just knew that she had to put the brakes on before things progressed too quickly. 'We got work tomorrow.'

He smiled, his teeth showing. 'Shame, I was just getting comfortable.' He kissed her forehead. 'Saturday, yeah?' He confirmed.

'Night, Jimmy.'

She peeled away and returned to Mel's room where she laid in the dark, wide awake with exhilaration, staring at the moon-spun shadows that danced across the far wall. The beating of her heart felt so loud, her blood pulsed through her temples on the side of her head in its virulent rhythm. She had no idea how she was going to get to sleep.

XIII

'Oh my god!' Mel hit Felicity with a pillow. 'No way. You little minx! You're a fast worker that's for sure.'

Mel had arrived home from work the following evening and Felicity could not wait to tell her what had gone on. All that day at the store, she had been in a daydream and had no one to share her tale with. Mel had received the complete works, full-bore, lock, stock and barrel, when they had finally come together.

Felicity felt like her face was going to split, her smile was enormous, threatening to split her face in two.

'Seriously, though, take it easy.' Mel's tone was one of kind advisory. 'I don't want you to get hurt.' Mel sparked a cigarette. 'Though, to be fair,' She blew out a cloud of smoke, waving her hand to disperse the fog. 'I do think he's taken with you. I've known him a while and he's never shown any interest in anyone else. Not even Jan.' Mel gave some consideration. 'Mind you, Jan tends to choose her own muse and they don't normally have much choice in the matter!' She chuckled.

Felicity sighed. 'It's weird. It just felt really comfortable, I liked spending time with him. We're going out together at the weekend.'

'Flick,' Her eyebrows were raised in mock disbelief. 'The weekend is tomorrow!'

It was hard to believe that Felicity had lodged in the house for nearly a week. In that time, she had worked five days in her new employment, met some new friends, started a romantic liaison with a skinhead and had her hair cut by a local bovver girl!

'Anyway, I've also been dying to tell you something.' Mel sat forward conspiratorially. 'I had a chat with Alexis,' Mel stopped herself. 'Hold on, how stupid of me, you don't even know who Alexis is, do you?'

'French bloke, lives at the top of the house. Likes punk music.'

Mel nodded in approval. 'Oookay, Miss Marple, you've done some sleuthing.' She dabbed the remains of the fag out. 'Anyway, our studious French friend is heading back to France for the summer break and, guess what?' Felicity could not guess; she shook her head lightly.

'He has agreed that you can shack up in his room for the summer if you are happy to cover his part of the rent.'

Felicity jumped on Mel wrapping her arms around her tightly. 'You're the best, Smell!' She planted a big smacker on her friend's cheek then, in mock disgust, wiped the smear of pale foundation from her lips.

*****

For the second time in just under a week, Felicity sat at the top deck of the Routemaster bus, only this time she was heading back in to the city. Quiet had let her sit by the window so that she could see the sights as they travelled, he was content enough with sitting beside her, his long arm draped across her shoulders, his fingers twiddling with the feathery tails of her hair.

Mel had gifted her a denim jacket that she rarely wore. Felicity had offered to pay for it but Mel had joked that it was a good luck jacket and she wanted her to have it. 'You look like a proper skinhead now.' Mel was jesting but it was true. The jacket looked great with her feather cut.

Felicity fiddled with the flap of the breast pocket and the little red tab that stuck out from it. It was nicely fitted, the hem sitting just on her waist. Mel had let her borrow the jeans, vest and boots again though she knew she would need to buy some things of her own. She had tucked some of her wages in to the breast pocket. She kept checking to see that it was still there.

It had been huge moment for her at the end of her shift the previous afternoon, a definite rite of passage. She had almost left the shop's forecourt and turned confused when Mr. Chowdury called her back.

She had forgotten to collect her wages. When he had taken the notes from the till and had handed them to her, she had felt awkward, not knowing the etiquette or expectations that were in place.

Clasping her first ever earnings, all she had done was utter, 'thank you.'

Mr. Chowdury had replied that she had earned it and to 'have a lovely weekend'.

'See you Monday.' She had called back over her shoulder as she left. Her hard-earned secure between her palm and fingers as she skipped away and up the road.

That was yesterday. Today was Saturday and she was full of anticipation at what the day offered.

'Where do you want to go?' Quiet had asked her before they had set off.

'I want to see the Thames, the river.'

He had grabbed her hand as they left the house. 'If that's what Feathers wants to see, that's where Feathers shall go. The old River Thames it is then.'

A ten-minute walk to a busy crossroads in Dalston and a short wait at the bus stop was all it had taken to start their travels. Now they were sat on the top deck, as the bus chugged along Kingsland road, a long straight run that seemed to go on and on. A very busy thoroughfare that sliced through both types of Hackney, poor and affluent, expensive-looking town housing nestling in close proximity to blocks of utility-styled council housing. Merging with Shoreditch High street, the bus had to stopping frequently to allow passengers on and off. She looked down at the broth of human life; creatures of all shapes and colours going about their business. Without much of a fanfare. Shoreditch became Norton Folgate. The name was peculiar to her, a short run in to Bishopsgate. Felicity loved the clash of architecture, the new and shiny grafted on to the old and crispy.

'Where we are now is called Bishopsgate because it was one of the original eight gates in the London Wall.' Quiet gave her a guided tour. 'The road was actually here before the Roman's built the boundary wall.' In his element, Quiet continued. 'It's amazing to think that we are travelling on a road that has run through here since before then, ain't it.'

'It is.' She agreed and snuggled back in to his arm.

Bishopsgate was a long stretch, dwarfing the previous Norton Folgate by some length. At a busy interchange, Bishopsgate became Gracechurch Street which did a big righthand swerve at Eastcheap, fiddling around the houses a bit until the bus entered Lower Thames street. She gave Quiet a little smile of recognition which he returned with a squeeze. It tickled him to see her excitement.

Lower Thames became Upper Thames. 'We're travelling alongside the river now. Won't be long.'

Veering down in to Blackfriars underpass, Quiet got up. "Come on Flick.' Felicity swung round and joined him. They shuffled down the aisle, Quiet jabbed the red button, an audible ding telling the driver to pull in at the next stop. It was during that momentary wait that she noticed something that she had not been aware of before. It was mostly the subtle movements or behaviour that alerted her. Passengers seemed to look away when she caught their eye. There was something deliberate about it, as if they were being careful not bring attention to themselves. A women appeared to pull her small child in closer. It suggested a nervousness, almost a fear.

Though she was alert and noticing all manner of things, Quiet was quite oblivious to the other passengers. He tugged her along by the hand, making his way down the stairs to the rear platform where they stepped off on to London's Victoria Embankment. He leaned down and kissed her on the lips. 'I hope you had your Weetabix, we've got a good hike ahead of us.'

As the bus pulled away from the stop, she looked up through the belch of diesel exhaust. Eyes, uncertain and unsmiling, stared down at her.

******

Following the river upstream, stopping occasionally to take in the view across the wide expanse, Felicity was in her element. Quiet was happy to follow in her wake as she darted from spot to spot, pointing out all manner of distractions, both on and off the water. He was rewarded for his patience with impromptu embraces and kisses. At an ice cream van, he bought them both a Mr. Whippy ice cream drizzled with raspberry sauce and speared with a chocolate flake. He laughed at her antics as she bit the bottom off her cone and tried to suck the ice cream through the hole.

They passed Temple station crossing the river to Southbank at Waterloo bridge. They stopped mid-river to gaze down its length. A homeless woman shuffled past them swathed in numerous outer garments; jumpers, woolen cardigans, at least two overcoats. She was elderly and filthy dirty. She carried a number of carrier bags stuffed full of more clothing. Felicity wondered how she coped with all the weight. The woman was laden like a mule. The woman stopped by them.

She stared hard at Felicity through black eyes that had seen too much of life. Deep lines etched her face like the bark of an old oak. A headscarf shiny with grease framed her head.

Felicity looked to Quiet for reassurance. He reached in to his jeans and handed the woman a coin. She lowered a handful of bags and took it from him. She slipped it in to her mac pocket without offering thanks continuing to stare at Felicity. Eventually she lifted a fingerless gloved hand, her index finger pointing. 'Pretty girl. You got pretty eyes.' Then she picked up the bags and walked away. Felicity watched the woman's stooped figure disappear across the bridge.

'C'mon, Feathers.' Quiet turned her shoulders.

Through Jubilee gardens they arrived at Westminster Bridge where they stopped for some time to allow Felicity to drink in the sights there including the grandiose riverside establishment, Parliament, the palace of Westminster. They bought a hotdog from another van for lunch and found a bench situated as close to the river as they could, where they sat for a long time in each other's arms, talking and watching the flow of river life.

She fell asleep on the way home, exhausted after the excitement of the day.

******

Quiet pushed the door open and stepped in to his room. 'You can come in if you want.' He reassured her. He walked over to the mattress and straightened the throw before flopping down on to it. His head propped up on a jumble of pillows and cushions. He sprawled along the length, his legs crossed at the ankles and his fingers linked across his groin. He still had his boots on.

Felicity looked around the room. As make-shift curtaining Quiet had hung a union flag. It made the room darker than normal but let enough light in for them to be able see. Beside the mattress a bedside cabinet was topped with a small desk lamp and a collection of beer bottles. A bone handled bowie knife, was tucked among the bottles. A small collection of books was piled within easy reach. A hardback, a biography about General Montgomery alongside a cheap, pulp paperback, Skinhead escapes by Richard Allen. A dark chest of drawers was tucked tight in to a corner, brass effect handles dangled from the drawer fronts. Felicity was surprised by how tidy Quiet kept his room. She could not help but be curious. Quiet's amused eyes followed her as she padded around his room. She went over to the chest of drawers.

She was drawn by the old-fashioned record player. It was covered in red vinyl that had lost some of its luster over the years. The corners especially were showing signs of wear and tear. A silver mesh was fixed to the front and on the right were three knobs. HMV lettering was positioned above a small red power light. 'It works'. Lift the lid.' Quiet encouraged, he got up from the mattress to help her. Felicity lifted the lid as he arrived at her side. Quiet leant down and flicked the power on at the socket. The little red light glowed brightly.

'Pick a record.' Quiet pointed to a small collection of LPs and 45s leaning against the skirting board.

Felicity began sifting through the LPs. Most of the bands in his collection she had never heard of but after a few seconds, she stopped, recognizing a band that she had seen on TV's 'Top of the Pops'.

Thursday evenings in the care home had always been highly anticipated. After tea, the lounge was always full of kids waiting for the opening credits to fire up. The sleeve of the LP was feathered at the corners, a sign that it had been played often. The seven band members, posed, some dressed in long coats, in front of a tube station entrance. One of them was hamming it up in the middle of the huddle, pulling a silly face and wearing ballooning, pinstripe trousers. Felicity lifted the LP from the stack and held it up for Quiet.

Madness – absolutely

Quiet gave a little chuckle and slipped the inner from the outer sleeve. He tugged the record free, handed Felicity both sleeves and placed it on to the turntable. There was a slight crackle and pop as the needle ran in to the grooves. Felicity recognised the song immediately. A raucous, fairground ride of sound, an homage to those boisterous schooldays.

Naughty boys in nasty schools
Headmasters breaking all the rules

Happy with her choice, she moved to the mattress and plonked herself there. Her attention turned to the sleeves. She had never owned a record, let alone a record player.

The sound was amazing to her. There seemed to be no gaps in the songs, no space, the orchestration packed to the seams with different sounds; saxophone, piano, guitars, drums. All working so perfectly together. The singer's vocals oozing with London vernacular and youthful dynamism fitted perfectly. She focused on the rear of the sleeve, reading the track listing then turning her attention to the blurb, sleeve notes written by a Sounds magazine journalist.

'We've had punk and funk, pub rock and disco. We've got mod and ska. So what's next then?'

'Get ready for the 'nutty sound' of Madness!'

A large illustration of a London underground roundel filled one side of the inner sleeve. Felicity knew that it was a fictional station, there was no 'Cairo East' station on any tube map she had ever seen.

Some of the names tagged at the bottom were odd; Suggs, Chas and Woody.

The first song ended and segued in to the next. Another that she was familiar with.

Received a letter just the other day
Don't seem they wanna know you no more

She moved with the music as she flipped the sleeve and learned about 'The birth of the Nutty Boys'. A clever family tree, illustrated with small photographs of the band members, filled the space. Felicity decided Suggs was her favourite. He was handsome and she liked his style.

She made herself more comfortable and slid along the mattress until her shoulders and back were supported by the cushions. She toyed with the LP sleeves, turning them over numerous times, enjoying the imagery, studying details and information. Felicity loved the clothing the band wore. Quiet had stretched out alongside her. He had folded his hands up behind his head. She could feel his boots tapping to the rhythm.

As each song ended and another started, she would check to see what it was called on the sleeve notes. The last song on that side was a rioting, rhythm and blues rocker called Solid gone. As a mechanical click was heard. Quiet flung himself up and turned the LP over.

'I love this tune.' He dropped back to the mattress turning on to his side, his head propped up, a hand pressed in to the side of his face. He seemed deep in thought, nodding his head in rhythm to the song. He sung along.

How come he enjoys himself not me?
How can she smile a good morning to me?
Felicity watched him, catching his eye.
How do they make a hard day's work easy?
Tell me something I'll put it to the test.

With his free hand, Quiet reached across and gently eased the LP sleeves from her hands. Felicity's felt the hairs stand up on her arms. She pursed her lips and held her breath. He eased himself over until he was close, leaning across her shoulder. He leant in and kissed her.

Felicity, submitted to the feeling of amorousness that flooded her limbs. She reached around his neck and pulled him closer until they were entwined. His tongue gently separated her lips and found her own. She followed his lead and allowed the dance to happen. It felt good and she immersed herself, swimming in the moment.

She could hear the record playing but the distraction was complete. She allowed him to run his hand down to her waist where he found the hem of her vest. Her stomach muscles rippled as his fingertips, rough to the touch but gentle in approach, found their way up to her bra. She let him slip his fingers over and beneath the cup where he found her breast. She sucked in air as he massaged her flesh and teased her nipple. She became more urgent, her tongue livelier and more searching. Quiet broke away and stood. His arousal was clear to see. He reached down and helped Felicity to her feet.

The pair stood silhouetted against a backdrop of red, white and blue.

Quiet reached for the hem of her vest and drew it up over her head. It snagged one of her hooped earrings, causing her to giggle. She freed the garment and dropped it on to the floor. Felicity placed her hand on his chest. Their eyes locked. Felicity let her gaze bore in to his eyes, searching. Into his soul she burrowed, exploring his very marrow, exploring his very being, looking for the reassurance that she was safe. Quiet held her stare. Not a blink broke.

She felt for the placket of his gingham shirt and undid the small buttons letting the garment unfold. She ran her hand over his bare chest, fingering the small laurel wreath logo tattooed on his left breast. Quiet shuddered as her light fingertips ran across his nipple, hard and erect. Daringly, she gave the nipple a pinch. Quiet closed his eyes and groaned softly. Felicity slid her hand down, back around his waist, pulling herself back in to his arms. She lifted her chin, inviting their lips to clash passionately once again.

XIV

It was pitch-black when she woke. The flag rippled gently at the window as the night breeze wafted in. Quiet was still sound asleep, sprawled on his front, prostate, his arm draped across her. She had woken on her side, her knees drawn up, her hands tucked under her chin, facing the far window wall. She lay for a while watching the flag dance and tried to enjoy the lick of cool air tickling her shoulder but she could not settle. Something disturbed her. A cacophony of noise rung out in her head. Images, none that made sense, appeared and disappeared, fast and furious, flashing across her mind. Her muscles twitched and protested, becoming increasingly taut, agitation prickled her skin. The once spacious room crept in on her, squeezing and sucking until she felt she was going to suffocate. She did not want to wake him.

She rolled herself from underneath his arm on to the floor and scrabbled around for her clothing. Unfurling her knickers she wriggled her slim legs into them then slipped the vest over. Clutching at the rest of her clothing and boots she eased the bedroom door and crept, bare foot, out on to the landing. She needed air. An invisible hand tightened on her throat threatening to cut off her airway. Her eyes widened; her skin tightened, fine hairs stiffened on her arms, her shoulders and her neck. What was going on? Was she ill? Was she suffering a heart attack of some sort?

It was a feat of real willpower that she was able to control the urge to run, to sprint through the house to the front door. Part of her brain demanded that she panic yet she found the restraint from somewhere. She dropped the bundle of clothing and boots at the bottom of the stairs and, stumbling, dizzy with panic, she almost fell in to the front door. She flung it open and stepped out on to the porch.

She gulped a huge lungful of the chilled night air. She found the top step and dropped down on to the cold concrete leaning back against the balustrade. The cold, rough aggregate quickly numbed her buttocks and it helped. The different sensation offered an unexpected relief of sorts, distracting her focus from the intense discomfort she was experiencing and replacing it with another form. She found the latter much more preferable.

She did her best to make herself comfortable, forcing her muscles to relax, to ease the irrational tension. She focused on the gate at the end of the foot-path. It took effort but she managed to regain some composure, her agitation slowly eased, her breathing slowing back to normal. She sat for some time, afraid to move back inside lest she trigger another episode. Intermittent flashes of white lightning burst in her head threatened to reignite whatever had dis-turbed her but she was able to extinguish them one by one until the sparks ceased.

It was only when she began to relax fully that tiredness began to creep back in to her being. The episode had drained her, it was as if she had sprinted a marathon. Her chin hit her chest as she nodded, dozing. Recognising that she was at the point of falling asleep on the porch she pulled herself up and head for her room at the top of the house.

Once there, she had a long, anxiety-induced wee, brushed her teeth and dropped on to her own mattress. As she settled, the effect of the chill began to set in. Shivering she pulled the bedding tight around herself creating a cocoon. She tucked her chin deep in to the ruck of material and allowed herself to drop off.

******

It was an effort to peeled her eyes open. When she opened them, Quiet was sat against the wall staring at her. He was bare-chested and bare-foot wearing only pair of army greens. His knees drawn up, his forearms resting across them. How long had he been there? Wearily, she rubbed her eyes. 'Morning.' She croaked.

'Is it?' He seemed disgruntled; she worked that out quickly. She unraveled herself from the bedclothes and propped herself up on her elbow.

'What's up?'

'I'm not sure, Flick.' Quiet gave his head a little shake. 'Yesterday I thought things went great. I had a really nice day, I thought you did too.'

'I did.' She reassured.

'Then we got back here, ended up in bed together, which,' He paused, 'I also really enjoyed. I wake up this morning and you've done a bunk.' He held his hands out questioningly. 'What was it? Too much, too soon? Or you de-cided that it was all a mistake? What? I'm confused.'

'None of them, you idiot.' She reached out to grasp his ankle. 'I couldn't sleep and didn't want to wake you up so I came up here so I could read with the light on. That's all.' She tugged at his ankle. 'Seriously, a mistake?' She giggled. 'The only one making a mistake is you! Getting hooked up with me!'

She pulled harder until he came away from the wall. She flung the bedclothes aside. 'Plenty of room in here for two!'

******

She had never had so much cash. Work was good. She ate well, had somewhere to crash and still had some spare to spend on what she wanted.

What she wanted was some clothes of her own. For once in her short life, she had the opportunity to go shopping for herself. She had been on shopping trips before when she had been at the home but those excursions had been only when necessary and always overly chaperoned. Controlled to the point of stifling non-expression. On those shopping trips she had been offered a glimpse of the latest fashions through the windows of the high street stores. Tight satin trousers, shiny velour jumpers. Sparkling boob tubes, flowing, flouncy necked blouses and slingback shoes; all beckoned her as she passed. But Felicity had been destined for the fashion of the dowdy. Her growth stifled by the confining parameters of what was deemed suitable attire for a girl of her years. Herded to the preferred outlets approved by the homes leadership team she found herself a prisoner of the limited garb on offer in those small, dark and musty boutiques of a by-gone era.

But that was then. Today was her day and she was going to have a blast. Quiet had suggested they head for the East End. She could tell he was fond of the area. Enthusiasm shone out of his eyes; a vibrancy seemed to light them up. 'You'll love it.' He had simply said.

They had hopped on the number 22 bus and as usual headed for the top deck. Felicity loved the vantage the position offered. She loved to people watch, curious about their movements and about their agendas as they went along with their daily lives unaware of her attentions. The changes in landscape, environment and architecture fascinated her. She recognised much of the route from her first day-out with Quiet but that day had been a bit of a blur. Today she felt so much more settled and was able to absorb more of the experience. Brick, stone and mortar provided a kaleidoscopic, textured background to the scenes below. Hues of deep browns, yellows, greys mottled the facades. Old London stock brick, naturally yellow but stained dark with years of pollutants mingled with the newer-breed Fletton bricks and concrete block. Gaudy bright signage, plastic and neon-lit, was slowly suffocating the once vibrant, wooden shop signs of the previous century. Advancing technology and the convenience of plastics were ensuring that the cherished trades of old, such as sign-writing, were becoming redundant.

They hopped off the rear platform at a crossroads. Quiet lead her briskly in to another wide and busy thoroughfare; Bethnal Green road. Felicity found herself among a heaving maelstrom of human activity. Quiet's tight grip on her hand prevented her from spinning like a top. The chattering exchange of greetings, dealings and exhortations was both familiar and mysterious to her, a proverbial molotov cocktail of London cockney and Bengali dialect.

She gawped in awe at the energy of the Asian community, short in physique yet tall in their exertions, they darted from one point to another, carrying out their daily routines as if all was to end tomorrow. Many of the men had combined their traditional clothing with western items; very loose fitting traditional Bengali bottoms, much like the pyjama bottoms worn by English men, swung high on ankles attached to sandal-clad feet often paired with an item of European fashion such as a suit jacket on the elders or big collared bomber jacket on the young bloods.

The Jews were still there, whose ancestors had followed the Huguenots and pre-dated the Bengalis; quiet and reserved in the most, some dressed observantly in black. Ancient Brits, men in tilted trilbies and shirt sleeves, women in summer dresses and sun glasses fingering orange-tipped cancer sticks gathered outside shops catching up on the local gossip. Youths, mixed in colour and culture, zig-zagged the wide paved paths, fooling around and chatting.

They passed Giorgi's café, busy inside and out; its sign left behind from a bygone era, advertising Players N0.6 cigarettes. The salty aroma of frying bacon, sausage and eggs mixed with the musty cotton-wool of fag smoke tickled their senses. By the time they turned in to Sclater Street, Quiet had given her a history of the East End's gangland past. They were close to Vallance road where the family home of the infamous Kray twins was. His animated enthusiasm for history amused her. His recalling of the twin's penchant for violence both revolted and stimulated her. She was listening but her attentions were locked in to the immediate rather than the historical.

Sclater street veered away from Bethnal Green road, narrower in breadth, hemmed in by tall, brick buildings of industry and trade. They followed the road until they reached the T-junction with Brick Lane. Quiet pulled her across the busy section, over the hustling bustle of the main thorough-fare, weaving through the gathered mass of Bengali locals and tourists and in to Cheshire street. Felicity followed his lead, unconcerned, secure in the knowledge that Quiet knew where he was going.

They arrived at the worn-out frontage of a small shop. P.Blackman, provider of men's footwear, a simple fact being that the single window was dressed from top to bottom with the black, browns, tans and reds of utility boots and shoes. Felicity resisted Quiet's tug towards the dusty, crusty window. "What the hell?" She wrinkled her nose in distaste.

'Trust me, Flick.' He chuckled, 'Have I let you down yet?'

Felicity gave him a playful punch to his stomach. 'This could be your moment of glory!'

Quiet lovingly cast his eyes over the variety displayed in the window, hung like the ornaments form a Christmas tree. He pointed out his favourite styles among the vast collection of different designs and different colours of the leather uppers. Airwair soled Dr Martens featured heavily among the side-gusseted dealer boots. Leather soled brogues and Gibsons hung alongside heavy work and combat boots. Wellington boots and plimsoles were plentiful and cheap.

He drew her attention to a smooth front shoe. Low cut with three lace holes, yellow stitching held the Bouncing sole. She liked them. There was a choice of colours, black or oxblood. She liked the oxblood, a deep, rich and warm shade of red, the color of the blood of an ox. Ox blood had historically been used as a pigment to dye fabric, leather and paint. The beast's blood would change from a bright red to a darker, oxidized, more brown-red as it aged. That almost certainly was not the way they were dyed nowadays but she loved the rich colour. She nodded in agreement with Quiet's recommendation.

He led her inside in to a claustrophobic sales area where stacks upon stacks of boxes threatened to topple and bury them for eternity. 'What can I do you for?' The salesman was unlike any sales assistant she had ever seen. He could have been someone's grandad.

She let Quiet speak on her behalf. It was easier. He approached with a familiar and capable air; she would not have known what to ask for. The man busied himself around them, he was incredibly efficient. He checked her sizing then scrabbled among a tall pile off boxes with not an ounce of concern for his personal safety. She was relieved when he teased a box from the tower without causing harm to himself or her and Quiet. He deftly laced them for her as she waited patiently. Passing them to her as if making an offering from the gods of bouncing souls. She pulled them on.

'They'll need a bit of breaking in darling. All new Docs are tough to start with.' He reassured her.

Quiet nodded in agreement at the man's advice. She stood up, looking down at the neat, flat laces and loved them instantly. So much so, that she insisted on keeping them on despite Quiet's concern that she may get blisters.

Stepping back out on to the street, Felicity kept looking down to admire her new shoes. Quiet slipped his hand back in to hers and led the way once again. Cheshire street was full of trade. Legitimately licensed stalls vied for passing custom, the wares piled high on wooden-planked market barrows. Among these well-established street outlets, in any gap or space that could be utilized sat street vendors, their offerings for sale spread invitingly on a roughly spread bedsheet or blanket. Quiet stopped to squat by a spread of bric a brac. He flicked through an untidy offering of old records; singles and long players. He found something of interest and separated the record from the Mantovani, Jim Reeves and Top of the Pops long players. Pleased as punch with his catch, a grin spread across his chops, he showed Felicity the cover. This is Desmond Dekker, the lettering bright orange with yellow highlighting. Desmond peered out from behind the leaves of a cheese plant, the record label Trojan, white in the top righthand corner. Quiet's little victory tickled her.

He bartered with the woman sat by the spread. The woman looked tired of life; her face expressionless and devoid of emotion. The barter was cold and functional. She could not be bothered and waved her hand dismissively. No pleasantries were exchanged between the pair. They agreed on twenty-five pence. Felicity wondered how this compared to the original fourteen and six in old money that the roundel stuck to the cover told her it had once cost. Quiet paid the woman and she shoved the coins in to her pinny front.

Quiet took her to a stall swathed in blue denim. Jeans and jackets hung high from the overhead steel rails on recycled hangers and covered the wooden display surface in a tangle of blues. Many different shades of denim crossed legs; Wranglers, Levis, Lee, Lois, Falmers, Lee cooper. Quiet dove in, happy to bang elbows with the other diggers as he rooted among the disordered piles like a man digging for diamonds. "What size waist are you?' He checked.

With effort he pulled a pair of straight leg jeans clear of the tangle. He checked the size and handed them over for her scrutiny. Worn but wearable, with some fading on the knees the Levi jeans looked to be in good condition. She held them against her waist. There was no option to try them on but they looked like a good fit. She nodded her approval. Quiet grabbed the stall holder's attention. A deal was struck and her purchase stuffed unceremoniously in to a re-used carrier bag. Quiet handed her the bag and draped his hand across her shoulders, making a noise like a caveman. 'Just call me hunter-gatherer man.'

They stopped at a stall selling apple fritters. Piping hot and dripping with cinnamon-sugar, it took all her patience to avoid burning her mouth on the sweet, energy-boosting delicacy. They sat to rest on an empty cart just off the main drag in a storage yard. Other spare carts, some in need of repair, dotted the yard. An overground train rumbled close by. Felicity was sure she spotted a rat sprint from one end of the yard to the other, hugging close to the bricked arches. The stop gave Felicity time to take in her surroundings. The space had been made useful, arches had been commandeered and put to use for storage. Quiet told her of the area's tribulations through World War II.

He reached across brushing sugar from her chin. He grabbed himself a cin-namon-sweet kiss.

She swung her legs beneath her. 'I'd like to get one of them tops.' She de-scribed to him, the collared polo tops with the laurel wreath chest logo; a Fred perry. He knew exactly what she meant.

He led them back out on to Brick lane, at Wentworth street they chucked a right hand and followed the road down to Goulston street. She was immedi-ately hit by the activity of youthful exuberance ahead. The Last Resort seemed to be the lure, its sign, illuminated in neon-blue tube lighting, hung inside the single store window. The façade around the big window was painted in a gaudy shade of blue. Heads lifted as many eyes checked their approach. Her paranoia bit hard, convinced that most of the attention was aimed at her. She was a stranger to them, an unknown. Their territorial pissings were threatened and they wanted to know who by.

Quiet instinctively felt her discomfort and he understood. A more prohibitive gathering of England's youth would have been hard to conjure up. Crop-headed boys and young men loitered dressed for street-maneuvers and fights. Nearly all were shoed in boots of different lengths and colours. Army greens, jeans and sta-prest trousers were coupled with button-down shirts and sports tops or t-shirts emblazoned with band logos; Ben Sherman mixing it with Fred Perry while Lonsdale duked it out with the mighty Cock Sparrer. The female contingent, teenagers mainly, clad much the same as the boys but with subtle adjustments, stood around chatting and smoking cigarettes.

Quiet seemed to grow beside her as they got closer, his chin lifted and he pulled his shoulders back. He gave her hand a firmer squeeze and walked con-fidently on. Those who knew him personally offered verbal greetings, hand-shakes and back slaps. Those less acquainted nodded in the old manner of mutual tolerance or respect, whichever suited.

Punk music blasted from the shop doorway while the gathered special brew hung around the shop front.

'Alright, Quiet?' A tall skinhead leaning against an empty stall, his hands thrust deep in his jean pockets called to Quiet. His black boots were laced in white, his t-shirt was printed with a band logo; 'Cockney rejects'. His forearms had been tattooed, one-piece flash; a panther clawed its way up one arm leaving thin red striations and the chunky crossed hammers of his beloved West Ham United decorated the other. 'Alright, Jez?' Quiet stopped to chat.

Felicity stood awkwardly at his side while the two men caught up. Absent-mindedly she began watching the boisterous antics of one group, smiling at the scene, as they play-fought up and down the street, wrestling each other to the floor and man-piling their victim. Clad for battle in boots, army greens, bomber jackets and jeans, an outsider may have feared the worse but there was no malice, just a handful of teenagers making fun on a warm summer's day.

The girls were well out-numbered by their male compatriots but Felicity caught the eye of two girls leaning on the sill of the store's window. As was her habit she allowed her eye to linger a moment too long. One of the pair stared her down through a wispy fringe. Arms crossed tight in defiance, the girl's Tonik suit jacket, three-buttoned with flap pockets, threatened to split at the shoulder seams. Fishnet tight-clad legs sprouted from a denim mini-skirt down to white socks and black shoes. Felicity offered a smile. The girl shrugged awkwardly and took a drag on a cigarette.

Quiet made to move on. 'Name's Flick, by the way.' She was annoyed by Quiet's lack of introduction.

'Hello, Flick.' He chuckled at her energy. 'Nice to meet you. Mine's Jez.' He gave Quiet a wink. 'Got yourself a good one there, mate!' Quiet gave a grimace. She let him lead the away satisfied that she had made her point.

They went in to the shop where she bought a black with yellow piping, Fred Perry, much to her delight. The shop specialized in attire for Britain's street culture; skinheads and punks mostly. The area had become a meeting ground for like-minded youths at the weekends. The window boasted a plethora of clothing and associated accessories that appealed to the sub-cults, the street-tribes who adopted fashions and music that separated them from the norm.

They stepped back out in to the sun-lit street. The crowd had thickened in the short space of time they had been in the shop. She felt Quiet's hackles rise and he seemed to hurry on. She resisted a little, she liked the vibrancy of the place and wanted to hang around for a while longer. ' C'mon Flick, Let's move on.' He hissed.

A voice cut through the crowd. 'Oi, oi, big man. Long time no see!' It halted Quiet in his tracks.

Felicity felt Quiet drop her hand. She looked to where the voice had come from. A confident, stout skinhead headed over. A cohort was at his shoulder, much slimmer than the caller but there was something spiteful-looking about him. Both had cropped heads, completely bald in slim skins case. Stout skinhead's t-shirt was decorated in the red, white and blue of the Union flag with a snarling bulldog at its centre; lettering young National Front across the chest. Skinny skinhead had chosen to keep his opinions to himself that day and wore a button-down shirt. Skinny looked to be the more troublesome of the pair.

'Hello Jack.' As they came together Quiet spoke first. Stout Jack clapped his hand hard on Quiet's arm in greeting.

'Not seen you in ages mate.' Jack seemed amiable enough. Felicity could feel the familiarity between them both, almost a brotherly atmosphere, certainly from Jack towards Quiet.

'You know how it is, been working loads. Doing some other stuff.'

'You've been missing out mate.' Jack continued while Skinny stood at his shoulder all the while staring hard at Quiet. 'Had a great bundle two weeks ago. Took the firm across the river to a little gig over there. The Thamesmead skins turned up and started giving it large. Mad ruck it was! Old bill turned up late to the party. All done and dusted by then. Thamesmead had it away on their toes!' Jack nodded towards Felicity. 'Who's this then?'

'Flick.' She decided to speak for herself. Quiet shot her a small sideways glance. She caught Skinny skin's roving eye and held it. Some would have called it a kind of sixth sense and it was this sense told her that Skinny was a bad egg.

'Nice.' Was all Jack offered in return. 'Anyway, don't be stranger. I miss our old catch ups.'

He held out his hand. Felicity watched as Quiet reached and shook. It looked begrudged and almost certainly was, that much she could tell. Quiet kept eye contact with Jack as their hands met. There was an atmosphere of test as they gripped each other. Felicity watched Skinny's cheek muscles tense. It was Quiet that broke away first.

'See you around, matey boy!' Jack moved away to mingle with others. Skinny gave a thin-lipped sneer then turned and followed. Felicity looked up at Quiet. His expression was blank as he watched the pair walk away. He looked at his palm then wiped it down jeans.

'Well, that was bloody weird!' Felicity broke the silence as they left. She had threaded her arm through his and squeezed in close.

'Always is.'

'Why? What's the problem with you two?'

'History. Nothing to get bothered about.' He pulled his hand from his bomber jacket pocket and put his arm around her. 'He's just some wanker I used to be mates with.'

'Used to?' Felicity's curiosity had been lit. 'What happened?'

'Difference of opinion really. We grew up near each other. Became skins at the same time. He was a good laugh, a good mate to be honest, we were tight.'

She waited for him to continue but was left waiting.

'I fuckin' hate politics.' Was how he left it.

XV

Felicity had only ever been to the cinema once. A trip had been arranged for the kids when she had been in the home. She was very young at the time but she could remember that it was 'The Jungle book' they had been taken to see. The film had been a delight to her, a welcome break from the confines of the home and the confines of her troubled mind. Bright, loud and energetic, the animated Disney production had offered just over an hour of pure escapism. King Louie's big scene was her favourite part, chaotic and mischevious, she had laughed at the ape's antics until tears rolled.

It was Quiet's idea. They had been heading home when he had suggested that they go to watch a film. They had jumped off the bus at Islington green where a small cinema was about to start its matinee showings. A quick perusal of the displayed posters and they had made up their minds. Quiet bought them both a ticket for the film; Raiders of the lost ark. They bought a big yellow packet of Treets, peanuts coated in a crispy, chocolate shell, to share and a paper cup of coke. He had convinced her to sit as far back in the cinema as possible. Other couples seemed to have the same idea and were amorously engaged before the lights went down. Felicity gawped as a pork-pie hatted rudeboy threatened to disembowel his rudegirl with his tongue.

Quiet elbowed her. 'Oi, dizzy daydream!' he chuckled, 'Stop staring!' He offered the bag of sweets. Felicity took a handful and threw them in to her mouth, just thankful that she had Quiet to help manage her naturally curious demeanor. It was a problem. She did not mean to be nosey or cause offence but living in the home had left her socially inadequate and naïve at times. She had not learned the art of restraint as yet. The lights dimmed and the curtains drew back. She took a gulp of coke, the ultra-sweet beverage helping her swallow the clot of chewed nuts and chocolate. Quiet leaned across and nuzzled her neck. She let him wander and explore for a few minutes, his lips found her own slippery lips as his fingers fumbled with the button of her jeans. She let him pop the button and slide her zipper down enough to let his fingers inside. She stopped him as he searched for her knicker elastic.

'Not here, Jim.' Was all she said. She could not see his eyes in the darkness but was intimate enough with his body language and atmosphere to know that he was okay with it. He whispered in her ear. 'I can't help it if you're such a sort, can I?' He kissed her and settled back in his chair to watch the film. She snuggled in close as he draped his arm across her shoulders ready for the action-packed swash and buckle.

******

Later that night Quiet pulled a crudely printed leaflet from his jacket pocket. She had noticed him pick it up in the Last Resort. She read it over the crook of his arm as the bus trundled homeward. It advertised a gig for a band called Offensive. The band had recorded an extended-play single cleverly called 'first offence', the gig was to be the promotional launch. The bands skinhead allegiances were obvious to see; the hair, clothing they wore. The leaflet displayed the four band members lined up, their backs to the lens, legs spread, hands cuffed behind their backs, under arrest. The rest of the blurb scattered across the sheet was gig details; where, when, why and how much. 'Are you going to go?' She looked at him, noticing the reflection of them both in the bus window. The bus interior lights were lit.

'Yeah, probably. They're good. Seen them support a band at the Bridgehouse a while back.' He stuffed the leaflet back in to his pocket. 'You fancy it?'

'Blimey! Bit public ain't it!' Her double entendre made him grin; she knew what he really meant and she would be going. He squeezed her close, playfully bit her earlobe and reminded her.

'You owe me! I've not forgotten, I've still not recovered from the knock back you gave me at the flicks!' He pulled her in to a playful headlock, rubbing his knuckles on her shorn scalp.

'You really know how to turn me on, you great girl's blouse!' She bit his belly in retaliation causing him to yelp. A middle-aged couple two rows ahead turned to look at their antics. Their disapproval was obvious.

'Call the vets!' Quiet fueled their disapproval. 'She's got rabies!'

******

'Typical thievin' Paki!'

Felicity stopped what she had been doing, the can of pineapple slices destined for the shelf now suspended in mid-air. She looked up to the convex security mirror. She could see two workmen at the counter. Mr Chowdury was behind but had stepped back as far as he could go against the racking. The man continued his tirade even as Felicity got up and walked over to them.

'I gave you a fiver not a fuckin' pound note! You've short-changed me!'

No sir, I am afraid you are mistaken. Your pound note is still here on top of the till drawer.' Mr Chowdury explained politely.

'Then you must have swapped it. Either give me my correct change or I'm going to jump over the counter and give you a hiding!'

'Mr Chowdury's not a Paki.' Felicity decided to add her voice to the debate.

Both men turned to look at her, both dusty and grubby from a day on site, heavy work boots on their feet. The bloodshot eyes of the agitated man stared her down. He spoke impatiently, his voice gruff. 'What?'

'I said, Mr Chowdury is not a Paki, as you so rudely called him. Or a Pakistani.' She made her point.

'So?'

'Well,' She replied a little sarcastically. 'If you are going to insult someone at least do it properly.'

'What the fuck are you on about?' The man shook his head and looked quizzically at his mate. 'Who the fuck is this mouthpiece?' He gesticulated with his thumb in her direction.

His mate shifted his weight, looking more uncomfortable by the second. 'C'mon Clive, let's go mate.' He tapped Clive on the arm, encouraging him to leave.

Clive was going nowhere. His anger grew, his temper welling up, his face getting redder, blood rushing to his head. It was a wonder he did not have a heart attack. He had been challenged and was not going to lose face to a stripling of a girl.

'I ain't going nowhere 'til this Paki gives me what he owes me!'

'You just don't get it do you?' Felicity puffed. 'Mr Chowdury is Indian. He's not from Pakistan, he's from India!'

'Again!' He bellowed. 'What's your point?'

Felicity raised her eyes in mock exasperation. 'How can he be a Paki, as you called him, if he's from India?'

'I don't fuckin' care where he's from, they're all the same. I just want my money!' Flecks of spit flew from his snarling vent. Felicity stepped back to avoid getting sprayed.

'All I can say is that if Mr Chowdury says he gave you the right change,' She shrugged. 'Then he did.'

'Well,' Clive's tone turned more menacing. All I can say is I'd prefer it if little bitches like you would keep your nose out of my fuckin' business. Anyway, what are you? A fuckin' dyke or something? What's with the hair? '

Felicity gave a look of mock shock. 'And I'd prefer it if fat bullies like you, went to school and learned something about the world rather than going around making nasty comments and causing trouble but we can't all have brains, can we?' She gave the man her best sarcastic smile to close.

He hit her, hard, right under the eye on her cheekbone. It was a full-bloodied blow, he did not hold back because she was a girl. She received the full weight of his building site strength and it sent her sprawling backwards up the aisle from where she had come from.

She was knocked scatty, her senses scrambled. Despite the verbal sparring, she had not expected things to escalate so dramatically. Now, she was vulnerable, sat on her backside in the aisle. She used the only thing she had to defend herself, a can of pineapple chunks. She hurled them at the man. She was as surprised as bully boy Clive when the tin found its target and bounced off his forehead. A thin slit opened. He frowned and dabbed at the area. He saw the blood on his fingertips and let out a huge bellow. He started towards her, his intent to do her more damage. A slap sounded.

It was so loud that it seemed to ring, ear splittingly sharp, around the shop interior but it had effect. It stunned all those within earshot. All eyes turned to the source of the sound. Mr Chowdury stood at the counter. In his hand, he held aloft, a machete. That which he had brought the flat blade down with such force on the counter surface. His knuckles white under the pressure of his grip, the blade glinting under the fluorescent light.

'Get the fuck out of my shop,' His voice now authorative, commanding, he bellowed. ' NOW!'

Clive was grabbed roughly by his mate. He did not need telling twice. 'Let's go before they call the Old Bill!'

Despite her injury, Felicity's blood ran cold at the mention of the police. She looked to Mr Chowdury.

'Are you going to call the police?' She fought to keep her voice calm.

Mr Chowdury shook his head, he stooped to tuck the machete away beneath the counter. 'Why? There is no point. They will do nothing.' He called out in Hindi.

Mrs Chowdury appeared and began attending to Felicity's swelling. She took a bag of peas from the frozen section and insisted that she hold them on the area. It helped.

You are a very silly girl!' She scolded. Felicity knew it was because she cared.

******

Quiet was livid. 'I will fuckin' kill them if I ever see them!' He ran his thumb over her bruised cheekbone. It had coloured up nicely, a good shade of blue. Thankfully, nothing appeared to be broken. 'You can't go around fighting everyone's battles, Flick! You were lucky not to end up in hospital.'

She tucked her head against his chest, fingering the buttons on his shirt. 'I didn't think I was fighting anything. Just doing what seemed right. 'She looked up at him. 'What would you have done?'

He sighed thoughtfully. 'I'm not sure, Flick.'

They laid there a while listening to music.

'Wonderful world, beautiful people'

'You and your girl, things could be pretty'

She held the record cover in her hands, a foiled psychedelic swirl around the title; Reggae Chartbusters. Various images of the same girl in different outfits, long dark hair, very pretty, decorated the sleeve.

'What really happened between you and Jack?'

He took his time responding. 'We knocked around together growing up. Lived really close to each other. He was a great mate, really loyal. He chuckled. 'He was a proper lad! I could tell you some mad stories. There was a time when we were running around the estate, think we were playing runouts or something, he though he was clever and climbed on to the garage roofs. Thought he could sneak to home without getting tagged! It didn't end well.' He chuckled at the memory. 'He fell through the corrugated roof! I did try to get to him but the roof was in pieces! He couldn't reach to pull himself out. In the end, we had to go and knock on the caretaker's door. He was the only person who had keys to the garages. He was not impressed! He got in so much trouble for that.'

The story made her smile. 'Sounds like you had a lot of fun together.'

'We did.' She felt the regret in response. 'Anyway, he started listening to stuff that the older blokes were always spouting off about. Problem with Jack is that he was never satisfied, always looking for something new, things more exciting. He tried to get me involved, but I couldn't listen to their shit. I didn't like them.'

'What couldn't you listen to?'

'Same sort of shit you heard today. Having a go at foreigners, blacks, Asians and that.' He let that settle a minute. 'Weird thing is we all hung out together when we were kids. I suppose its when we get older things change.'

He played gently with her feathers. 'Some of us choose our own way, Flick. I know who the real enemy is.'

'Take a look at the world'
'And the state that it's in today'
'I am sure you'll agree'
'We could make it a better way'

She did not press any further. It was clear that he found it tough to talk about. She was just pleased that he now trusted her enough to talk about things that were clearly emotional and awkward for him. She slid her hand between his shirt buttons, playing with the hair that snaked up from his pubic area. He gave a groan, lifted her chin and kissed her.

'This I know and I'm sure'
'That with love we all could understand'
'This is our world, can't you see?'
'Everybody wants to live and be free'

XVI

It was mid-week. Felicity had helped close up at the shop and had hot-footed it back to the house. Quiet had insisted that she be ready on time or be left behind. He had arranged a pick up. She knew he did not mean it and anyway, her excitement had intensified as the week had progressed threatening to turn her in to a whirling banshee. She had never been to a gig before and she had no intention of being left behind.

She had been to a pantomime at Christmas but quickly gathered that this experience would not be fairy stories with men dressed as women. She had endeavoured to apply the energy to her work in the hope that it would help her to stay calm. It had not worked. The Chowdury's could only stand and shake their heads at her chaotic flapping.

She grabbed residence of the bathroom early and was well in to her preparations when Quiet arrived back from his day at work. He popped his head in to say 'hello' and reminded her again what time to expect their lift then he disappeared to sort himself.

She hummed along with the melody as she pulled on the crisp button-down shirt she had bought from Jan. A bold, black and red tartan number that Jan could no longer button up around her expanding chest. The music cassette was the first she had bought for herself, from Woolworths record section. Quiet had spoken of the band and as they seemed to meet his approval, she had taken the plunge. The Specials were doing nothing.

People say to me just be yourself,
It makes no sense,
To follow fashion,

Gripping the waistband of her jeans, she wriggled and writhed them over her thighs and bum, tucking the hem of the shirt in and pulling the fly up. She waggled her legs to help them sit nice around her hips and crotch. They were a nice snug fit, showing off her attributes, she reckoned. Her white toweling socks really complimented the deep colour of her DM shoes. She tied them, making sure the laces were nice and straight and flexed her toes. They were breaking in, creasing across the front nicely. She checked herself out in the scabbed mirror screwed to the back of the door.

I'm just living in a life without feeling,
I walk and walk,
I'm dreaming,
I'm just living in a life without feeling,
I talk and talk,
Say nothing.
She gave herself a cheeky wink.

******

Raven was a real looker, really striking. He turned up bang on time and walked in uninvited. He was a regular visitor to the house and wandered in unannounced, finding Felicity waiting patiently in the lounge. She was keeping herself occupied attempting to roll a cigarette. She had yet to try her first smoke despite being surrounded by smokers of all shapes and sizes. It seemed to be the done thing among her new-found peer group but she was not overly curious about it. She was more curious about the art of rolling a cigarette than smoking one. She preferred the fresh smell of strands of tobacco in a pouch than having to inhale the fug of burnt tobacco. She was especially averse to the lingering stench of fag smoke-saturated clothing left overnight on the bedroom floor or the brown-sucked dog-ends that piled high in the ash trays. She looked up from her fumbling in to the bright eyes of Raven. Bright eyes set in a coffee-coloured, smooth face. His hair was around a number 2 crop, leaving just enough length to bleach peroxide yellow. It was a stunning and complimentary contrast. A gold hoop dangled from his left ear. He smiled, spreading full, glossy lips. 'Got a spare?'

Felicity offered him her creation. It was unique, that much could be said. Raven reached out and took the attempt from her. He chuckled.

'Shit! Nice trumpet! If I light that I'd be lucky to get one drag before it turned to ash. Looser than a whore's knicker elastic!'

He sat himself down next to her on the settee.

'I don't smoke really.' Felicity explained.

'I guessed.' Raven took time to deconstruct her attempt. She watched as he deftly slipped a new paper from the cardboard packet and spread the salvaged filling in to the new. His fingers weaved and rolled, his tongue deft across the glued edge, producing a neat and straight smoke. He lit the roll-up and sat back. He crossed a tightly-laced black boot up on to his knee. Felicity cast her eyes over his crisp, ice-white sta-prest trousers. Paired with a black button-down shirt finished with contrasting white buttons, he looked the business.

'You seeing Quiet then?'

'Name's Flick by the way.' She ignored his question, niggled that he had omitted polite pleasantries.

'I guessed as much.' He blew a plume of smoke up towards the high ceiling of the lounge. 'He's told me all about you.' A cobweb clinging to the corner coving fluttered, tempting a spider from its hole only to be engulfed in a chemical gas attack. 'Raven.' He gave a slight nod as introduction. 'So, Flick,' He over-pronounced her tag. 'How's things going with you and Quiet then?'

Quiet appeared in the lounge, a huge grin across his face for his friend. 'Hand's off she's mine!'

Raven lifted both palms in mock surrender. 'Good title for a song that!' He mock-whispered to Felicity. 'Better than inner London violence, I suppose!' He heaved himself up and dotted the fag out in the nearest ashtray before reaching down and pulling her up by the hand.

'Come on Flicketty Flick, let's go cause some aggro.'

******

Mel tripped in to the hallway still spraying her hair and teasing it into a huge candy-floss of rigid black. An acrid cloud of fog filled the area. Raven coughed and hacked theatrically. Mel displayed her sympathy by spraying him liberally as he escaped into fresh air.

Raven owned a car. It was not a rolls Royce but it was his and that was more than what could be said for many his age. His Hillman avenger was his pride and joy. He knew every scab, scrape and dent on its ten-year old body. A flat yellow with a black vinyl roof, it was his love. He reached over the back of the driver's seat and released the door buttons to let the girls in to the rear. Quiet fiddled with the front passenger seat causing Felicity to protest loudly as he sent the seat sliding back in to her shins. 'Can't help it if I'm lanky, can I?' That was Quiet's apology.

'Cut your bloody feet off.' Mel retorted. "You great streak of piss!'

Quiet began clattering about in the glove compartment as Raven fired up Hilda the avenger. He was sorting through a clutch of homemade cassette tapes, reading the spine and discarding those he did not fancy. 'We'll be there by the time you choose the soundtrack!' Raven pulled the car away from the curb.

Quiet slotted his choice in to the car stereo. Jimmy Pursey's gritted howl filled the car.

So, you wake up every morning,

Just to work and face yourself,

The warm evening air and the car's vinyl seating combined to give off a not unpleasant pungent aroma. Felicity certainly preferred that to the plumes of nicotine-laced smog that soon replaced it. She wound the window down to let some air in to clear the smokey interior. Quiet was nodding quickly along to the tempo, tuning in to Sham 69's punk assault. Raven was drumming his fingers on the steering wheel. Conversation was difficult. Felicity had to shout. 'Never been to a gig before.'

Mel leaned across the back seat. 'Then you're in for a bit of an adventure!'

******

They drove under the Thames River using the Blackwall tunnel. Felicity glanced up to the plaque that celebrated the opening of the tunnel by Mr Plummer in 1967, her eyes widened as they entered the brightly-lit worm hole. 'Get your passport ready,' Raven chirped. 'We're entering bandit country. Keep 'em peeled!'

Jimmy Pursey struggled to compete as the rush of noise inside the car increased, road noise bouncing off the tunnel walls and back in through the open windows.

So think before you do what they say,
It's your life so go your own way,
Questions and answers, honesty, lies,
Yes, no, you can't but you can if you just try.

Arriving in Lewisham, they parked as close as possible to the gig venue, a pub that boasted a large frontage. Youths already swarmed the area. Most had short hair and wore boots, among them the odd parrot plume of punk. The crowd milled, swigging pints of lager and pulling on cigarettes. They quickly found their crew among the crowd. Jan, Peanut and Micky were already present as well as a couple of new faces Felicity was introduced to. Quiet had learned his lesson and was quick to do the introductions. Felicity complimented Jan on her choice of jacket; a bright red Harrington, zipped three quarters, collars laid flat showing the tartan lining and allowing her button-down shirt collars to be displayed. Jan showed off her new monkey boots, brown leather, ankle length with a low flat sole. Felicity noted them down on her mental shopping list.

They entered as a group, Felicity tight to Quiet. The atmosphere inside was both vibrant and intimidating. Her friends seemed to take it in their stride, familiar with the etiquette required, unwritten but sacrosanct. A code of nods and eye contact. She was relieved to find Quiet's hand feeling for her own. It was as if he could sense her anxiousness.

The group made for the bar where Quiet elbowed himself a route through the tangle of tattooed arms and testosterone that swarmed over the beer-sticky dark wood counter. This confidence he carried served to make him all the more attractive to her. He reached out his long arm, a five-pound note waggling between his index and middle finger.

'Yep?' She demanded. The bar lady had no time for chit chat. All pleasantries had been dispensed with. She was clearly a veteran. An old-time rocker with dyed black locks, a ring in her nose and a Black Sabbath t-shirt that had clearly seen more gigs than most of the clientele had changed their own underwear. Quiet gave her his order, checking with Jan and Raven what they were having then turning to Felicity. 'What you having, Flick?' Felicity had difficulty absorbing the simple question. Sensory overload was kicking in and a barrage of distractions; sounds, smells and body contact threatened to turn her in to an anxiety-riddled amoeba. She focused back to Jan. What had Jan ordered?

'Snakebite and black please.'

Quiet chuckled. 'Not sure that's a good idea, Flick.'

Felicity gave him no quarter, no space to offer his reasoning. 'Snake bite and black.' She repeated. He frowned at her insistence.

'Ain't got all day mate!' The bar lady insisted. 'You'll get me lynched if this lot have to wait much longer!'

Jan intervened. 'Let her have what she wants, Quiet. It's her night out too.'

Quiet paid up and handed Felicity the cocktail of lager, cider and blackcurrant juice. 'Take it easy, Flick. We've got all night.'

He kissed her forehead and took a long draught of his lager. She turned from the bar and stuck her top lip in to the pint taking a tentative slurp. She liked it. It was sweet and moreish. She went straight back in and took another gulp. Jan laughed at her.

They headed towards the dancefloor. A good size crowd were already congregating in front of a very low stage area. Mic stands held front stage backed up with amplifier stacks and a drum kit. The bass drum skin had been customized with the band's name. A backdrop had been hung behind the set-up, a simple bed sheet spray-painted with crude artwork; a skinhead figure staring out from behind prison bars, the band's name; Offensive, beneath the image. They found a spot where they could hang out, chatting and joking among themselves and catching up with others that they knew among the crowd.

Felicity felt herself relaxing. Her muscles loosened and a warmness began to flow around her limbs. She could not help but grin. Early inhibitions eased away and she found herself more and more immersed in the moment. She joined in the conversations and laughed at the group's antics. She swapped banter with the lads and did her best to mimic Jan as she joined her and Mel dancing along to the PA system playing old-time reggae songs while the crowd waited for the band.

I told you once and I told you twice,
Wha' sweet nanny goat a go run him belly good,
Me said ah it mek, mek yuh pop yuh bitta gal,
Ah it mek while you accidently fall,
Ah it mek hear she crying out fe ice water

Jan was a great mover, eliciting glances from boys and glares from the girls. Felicity did her best to follow her lead. The alcohol had worked its magic and she was enjoying the freedom that the intoxication allowed her. All the while, Quiet watched over her antics, alert and protective, smiling at her exuberance.

Felicity made no protest as Jan squeezed another pint of the lethal brew in to her paw just as someone took to the stage, grabbed a mic and tapped it, interrupting the PA with a loud thudding. The noise quietened the crowd down. Felicity felt the surge as other punters pushed their way in to the gig area from the front bar. Quiet draped an arm over her shoulder and across her chest, holding her close in front of him.

'Good evenin' all you 'orrible urchins and tacky 'erberts!' The greeting was met with a raucous cheer. 'Let's have a huge South London welcome for the band the media love to hate.' He held out his arms wide. 'Let's fuckin' hear it for your band, not theirs; Offensive!'

The band clambered across the stage. The shaven-headed lead singer was amped, bare-chested in jeans and boots, he strangled the mic stand as he waited for the lead guitarist and bass player to plug in. His nostrils flared and his sinewy arms flexed as he barely contained his energy. The hum of feedback buzzed and crackled as the dials were cranked up to max. He rocked back and forth like a demented inmate, took a glance over his shoulder at the drummer, then with a screeched 1-2-3-4 count off, they exploded.

Felicity had never felt heat like it. Bodies swayed and crashed left and right. Arms and heads tangled and clashed as the band's energy evoked a furious display from the crowd. Tight and aggressive the band thundered through their set, the lead singer conducting the crowd, fueling the youthful exuberance and chaperoning when the exuberance threatened to erupt in to violence.

Felicity could only watch with amused amazement at the commotion around her. Despite the jostling she felt safe and laughed out loud as she watched her friends, Peanut, Raven and Micky join the riot of bodies close to the stage. The heat made her thirsty and she gulped at the sickly-sweet booze a little too urgently.

Then it was over, the band left the stage and joined some of the punters at the bar. Felicity felt like she had been spun in a whirlwind. Clammy sweat clung to her forehead, her mouth was furry and dry. She felt the room begin to sway and she struggled to focus. Quiet picked up on the signals. He clasped the back of her arms to keep her steady. He was talking to her but she could not hear him over the loud buzzing in her ears, her eardrums throbbed. All noise had meshed together, becoming a burble, a bubbling drone. Jan looked over and saw Quiet trying to support her friend. Felicity smiled at her stupidly; her eyelids droopy. 'Hello Jan!' she drawled. Felicity felt her stomach stew. She belched and smacked her lips.

'Fuckin' hell. She's going to be sick.' Jan stepped in and wrapped an arm around her waist. 'I'll take her to the bogs.' Jan dragged Felicity to the ladies' toilets where she squeezed her in to an empty cubicle, draped her over the toilet pan and encouraged her to put her fingers down her throat. Felicity laughed at the suggestion but Jan insisted. Felicity did what she was told and was soon vomiting loudly, spilling deep red spew in to the white ceramic bowl. Jan left the cubicle.

As the remnants of her stomach were purged, some focus began to return. After a few minutes her head had cleared enough for her to lift herself in to a sitting position, she fought to regain some composure. She blinked herself in to the present.

'You're a fuckin' slag.'

Felicity frowned and zeroed in. She was unsure that she had heard correctly and listened more intently.

'Think you can come over here and flaunt yourself at my bloke? You fuckin' cheap tart!'

Felicity did not recognize the voice but it was close, just outside the cubicle she was in. It was an agitated bark issued with intent. Felicity felt her blood run cold, concerned that the tirade was meant for her. A lot of the night had become a blur after the first pint of snakebite. A small reminder of her indulgence, acidic and burning, lurched in to her sore throat.

'What are you on about?' Felicity immediately recognised Jan's voice responding to the other. Her interest spiked quickly turning to concern for her friend. 'Why the fuck would I be interested in your bloke?' Jan continued.

'What you fuckin' saying? You mouthy bint!' The other girl was now clearly offended, her agitation rising. 'My bloke not worthy of your attention, you stuck up cow?'

Jan's following laughter sounded exactly as it was intended; mocking. 'You want to make your mind up! Either I'm a desperate slapper chasing your bloke or you're upset that I don't find him in the least bit attractive! Which is it, fuckin' enlighten me!'

'You think you're something special. Always acting like you're better than the rest of us. Walking around like your shit don't stink!'

Felicity could almost hear Jan shaking her head in disbelief. She stood and steadied herself reaching for the sliding lock on the toilet door.

Jan responded to the girl's challenge. 'You are one paranoid bitch! Why don't you get out of my face? You come in here with your mates, to what?' She questioned. 'To give me a hard time? To scare me?' She gave a short laugh. 'Sort yourself out why don't you!'

Felicity opened the door inwards. The mouthy girl was stood with her back to the cubicle confronting Jan; a very short crop-cut bristling on top of a crew-neck t-shirt, feathers only to her fringe, none to the rear. Two other girls had joined the girl in support. Any exit from the now cramped toilet was blocked. Felicity took a moment to assess. The feeling of imminent threat seemed to have a speedy sobering effect on her. It was clear that the group of girls that had cornered Jan meant malice. All the signs pointed to aggro. Aggro in a hard confined space.

'Sort myself out?' The main aggressor flexed. 'I'll fuckin' sort you out, you bitch!'

Felicity switched, her eyes widened, lucid and alert. She reacted instantly as the girl raised her fist. Felicity rammed her fist crunching in to the rear of the girl's bristly cranium. The sudden, unexpected impact sent the girls head shooting forward before it collided with poor old Jan's nose. There was a sickening crunch of bone on bone. An explosion of blood erupted from Jan's nostrils. Felicity gave no quarter. She clubbed at the girl again, a sideways blow from behind that cracked hard in to the girl's right cheek bone.

There was an audible crack, it was difficult to tell whether it was the crack of cheek bone or her own knuckles. The girl crumpled to her haunches but Felicity was not finished. She brought her heel down upon her upper back leaving a grimy, piss-wet shoe print on her t-shirt. The girl was lucky, she had been aiming for her head. The girl's gang screeched venom, clambering over their fallen friend to get at Felicity.

She met them head on, swinging both hands wildly but she was overwhelmed and staggered backwards, back in to the cubicle she had erupted from. The floor was slippery with urine and vomit, she fell. She found herself jammed between the toilet pan and the side wall of the cubicle. Both of her attackers went in to overdrive winging blows and trying to bring monkey boots and loafer heels down on her. Felicity covered her head and fended off blows with her legs. In desperation to get to her, the girls clashed as they attacked, their blows losing velocity. Felicity came to no serious harm but still, she was unable to find an opportunity to escape from the squeezed in assault.

As she resigned herself to receiving a prolonged beating, one of her assailants was hauled backwards from the cubicle. Jan had recovered sufficiently to add her argument to the bundle. The remaining girl was distracted by Jan's intervention, awarding Felicity a gap in the attack to heave herself up and to drive her head in to the girl's chest. The girl fell backwards over her fallen comrade and ended up in a heap beneath a sink opposite. It was her turn to feel trapped and vulnerable, the girl had the good sense to protect her face with her hands as Felicity swung her heavy shoes at her. A hard tug on her arm startled her. She turned, ready to attack. It was Jan.

'Come on. We're done.' Jan hissed, urgent and serious. She pulled Felicity away and out of the toilets. They moved quickly through the crowd towards the huddle of their crew, avoiding questioning stares from other punters.

'What the fuck's happened?' Mel grabbed Jan's shoulders. 'You look like you've been in a war!'

Concern etched Quiet's face. He recognized the signs of a good punch up.

'Size of that egg on your nut!' Peanut admired a lump that was appearing prominently from Felicity's scalp.

Jan's head was down. 'I think dey broke by dose.'

'I think we might get more than a broken nose if we hang about much longer.' Quiet was scanning over the group's heads. He spotted one of the girl's exit the women's toilet and alert a group of her friends; a sizeable group of skinheads and other toughs. He quickly recognised that they were outnumbered and away from home, the odds were not good.

He watched as the group mustered and began to move towards them.

'Move!' He ordered, spinning Felicity, Jan and Mel easily and setting them off towards the pub exit. Peanut, Micky and Raven were already moving, grabbing improvised weapons that might be needed if battlelines were met; a beer bottle, a leg torn from a stool. Luckily the pub was beginning to empty after the band had finished. They were soon through the bar area with Quiet bringing up the rear. As a last ditch defence, he pulled a table across behind them as they went, sending glasses, bottles and beer cascading on to the floor. It would not slow their pursuers for long but it was the best he could do in that moment. They hit the outside running, heading for the parked car, Quiet and the other boys hauling the girls along. A cacophony of splintering wood and battle cries erupted as the posse sent the table crashing through the pub entrance, clambering over the remains and flying up the road after them.

Raven was thankfully quick with the doors. Felicity, Mel, Jan, Peanut and Mickey piled themselves in to the rear seat, all grace and decorum left behind in the pub. The car lurched away in a belch of exhaust, the passenger door swinging like a wounded bird wing leaving Quiet grasping desperately to the car's roof gutters. His legs flailed away beneath him as he attempted to keep up with the accelerating car.

The girl's screamed at Raven to stop to let Quiet on board but he seemed not to hear, his concentration on the getaway. There was a graunch as the exhaust crunched in to the road surface, sparks and grit flying from beneath the car's over-laden back end. A bar stool thudded off the rear screen. Felicity turned panicked, to see the hoard of hooligans running at full pelt behind the car. Glass exploded all round. She screamed out at Raven to stop.

Quiet had other ideas though. He went for broke. Unable to keep the pace, his feet left the ground. With a huge do or die effort he swung his hips sideways and bundled in to the passenger seat, knocking Raven off-course. Raven fought the steering wheel and regained control as Quiet captured the swinging door before it tore itself off its hinges and slammed it shut. Raven gunned the straining motor pulling them away from the pursuit. Felicity breathed once more as the chasing mob disappeared from view.

'Well,' Breathlessly, Quiet broke the stunned silence. 'That was fun, weren't it!'

XVII

The weekend had arrived with the added bonus of the Monday being the August bank holiday. The usual crew had met up earlier that morning and were headed for the coast. The Essex coast; Southend on sea to be precise. By all accounts It was a destination that seemed to be hold some sentiment for her friends. She had enjoyed the build-up, the excitement and the anticipation among her friends, as the weekend drew closer.

The boys were their usual boisterous selves. They were finding it difficult to sit for long. Up and down the aisle they went, playfighting, monkeying around and generally annoying fellow travelers with their antics. It was early in the day but already alcohol was flowing. The train carriage was fuggy with cigarette smoke despite the windows being wide open.

Quiet was sprawled out, his legs across her lap. She was sat by the window watching the blur of the countryside as the train headed out towards the coast. Occasionally she felt him jerk with laughter at the others antics. Raven was sat opposite them; he had brought along a small cassette player. It was perched on his lap, the volume set at a respectful level by his usual standards. He jerked his head in time to the music.

I love you, yes i do
'Cos i know that you love me too
I love you, yes i do
Gonna spend all my money on you

Ska music, upbeat and vibrant, brass-laden, fitted the mood of the crew, Buster's croon perfect for the moment. She had no idea how long the journey would take and had no preconceived ideas of what to expect when they arrived. At that moment, it was enough that she was happy. Happier than she could ever remember being. These people had become more than friends. To call them family felt clichéd but it was hard to think of a more appropriate description. The fondness this small core group of individuals had for each other was not something spoken out loud or written anywhere. It was there in their actions, the way they carried themselves round each other. They were comfortable and free to be who they wanted to be. Disagreements among the group were frequent but rarely long-lasting. Occasionally they could become explosive but were settled quickly and laid to rest. Support was not asked for nor expected but freely awarded, without question or judgement. Loyalty was earned.

Most of the crew were skinheads and this was the initial common ground. This was how they had gravitated towards each other. But important as the cropped hair, the denims, the MA-1 flight jackets and boots were; the reality was that their bond was deeper.

Mel was not a skinhead and yet she was clearly an integral part of the group's foundations. In fact, it would have been hard to imagine the group without Mel's mother hen presence, her over-seeing manner and big sister advices.

Yet Felicity could not deny that becoming a skinhead had allowed her something that she had never fully appreciated before. The only previous identity she had reluctantly absorbed was that of a looked-after kid. Her time in the home had been one of compliance and adherence. In many ways, it was easier. Her daily life held little surprise, one of knowing. Knowing what to expect, knowing what was expected. What to do, what to say, what was going to happen.

What to wear.

And yet, instinctively this had never sat well with her. Something inside her had always looked beyond her circumstance, a strong need to assert herself.

When Jan had cut her hair, it had been akin to leaving behind a part of her that did not belong. A long tolerated, but hated, weight of experience that she had not asked for nor wanted to remember. For Felicity, getting her feathercut had been day one of the rest of her life.

She gave Quiet's knee a stiff rub. In return he reached across and knuckled her prickly scalp.

I don't care, when they stare, at the way that I'm always with you
We're a pair, it's not fair when they say we're a special brew!
Woh woh woh woh

At that moment, she had everything she needed.

******

As the train slowed, a chimp's chorus of screeches, cheers and bellows filled the carriage. Eager youths stood and clambered on the seats before the train had stopped. Felicity could see a swarm of cropped heads as far down the aisle as she could see. Doors opened and spilt the hoard on to the platform. Quiet swung his long legs around and slipped his fingers through her own. They joined the throng shuffling down the aisle. Raven turned to face them a big grin etched across his face.

'Are we there yet, dad?' He quipped. Quiet gave him a friendly shove.

The skinheads shuffled through the station eventually pouring out in to a wide-open frontage. Taxi drivers waiting patiently in the ranks stared out at the melee, fags dangling from dry lips, elbows hooked over open windows, contempt oozing from their twisted sneers. The station forecourt was teeming with youthful exuberance. An exuberance that was hemmed in and checked by a sizeable police presence. Bobbies stood in groups; arms folded in mild amusement at the sight before them. German Shepherd dogs strained at their handler's leashes, long pink tongues hanging out of long-fanged mouths, dripping saliva at the scent of some much-anticipated sport.

The route to the seafront was to be controlled, the local constabulary having been awarded the very dubious honour of escorting the rabble through the town. With some direction the crowd moved off, encouraged to hold ranks by the bark of the boys in blue and their furry enforcers. The atmosphere was generally good natured, banter being swapped between the skinheads and the accompanying officers as they went on their way.

'Lend me your hat.' A common request. The police officer, the receiver of the request respectfully declined.

'Does your mother know you're here?' An officer quipped.

'Nah, she's in prison!' The skinhead grinned.

It was not long before the muddy aroma of salt and seaweed filled nostrils and heightened senses, the sea was close by.

Felicity struggled to get her bearings but her instincts told her that they were being led parallel to and away from the main seafront. Noise among the crowd grew as more individuals became suspicious. Dissent grew, mutterings filtering through the crowd. It seemed they were being shepherded to an area where they could be managed.

Jostling began. Frustrated youths bobbed and weaved as they sought opportunities to give their escorts the slip. The dogs became more agitated, snarling and snapping at the shins of those unlucky enough to be in reach. It was soon very clear that there were not enough escorts to manage such a large crowd. Ranks were broken and small groups peeled off. The long arm of the law grabbed at collars and attempted to maintain some sort of order but it was a futile task. Like a game of Kerplunk, the youths dropped and rolled, spinning free, escaping the clutches of the bobbies. Felicity scooted after Quiet, his hand firmly clutching hers as he and the rest of the crew took their leave and broke away slipping in to a side street. Their escape was easy, with no pursuit they quickly created distance between themselves and the main crowd.

As if possessing an inner compass Quiet led their group down a long road that on first impression seemed to head nowhere until they emerged from between the two high flanks of houses and out in to the bright, open and inviting seafront; the great yawning span of Southend beach. The tide was way out, the sea sucked out beyond the estuary, leaving behind the glutinous silty mud flats that were home for the cockle beds that provided local sea food stalls with the small gritty mollusks' day trippers loved to eat. Felicity turned to Quiet. 'Where's the sea?' It was one of the things she had been most excited about seeing.

'Tide here goes out a long way.' Quiet reassured her. 'But it comes back in fast. It will be back soon'

They all turned right and joined the meander of the masses along the front. The pavements were alive with families making the most of the bank holiday. Ice cream-smeared toddlers swung around sun-burnt thighs evoking yelps of displeasure from mums. Dads ambled along sucking on Benson and Hedges, their vests struggling to contain their voluminous white beer-bellies. Grannies dug in purses, dishing out coppers to spread palms, their grandchildren eager to test their luck on the penny fall machines in the sea front arcades.

They regrouped at the Kursal, a once proud building, boasting high arched windows topped off with a tall imposing dome that stood tall overlooking the junction. In a state of decline, the building was now in little use. Its amusement park had long ago closed, the ballroom had closed as recently as 1977 and there was little left of the original charm the building once offered. It did however signal the start of the main promenade towards the famous Southend pier.

Skinheads were everywhere, in couples and in clusters scattered along the route. They stopped for a while, gathering on the low sea wall. A crowd had already congregated there and the crew seemed to know them well. They hung out there for a while swapping stories in between swigs of cider from passed-around bottles. There was talk that the local pubs were not serving skinheads, imposing a temporary ban. The quickly knocked-up door signs and hastily hired bouncers said so. She perched herself on the wall, scuffing at the sand blown on to the promenade, content to sit and watch the world go by while Quiet caught up with a couple of old friends. A daring passer-by stopped to take a photograph of the group. Peanut and Micky acted up for the camera, clowning around and pulling monkey faces.

The group moved on to the narrow strip of sand that led down to the mud flats and wandered along the beach. Sand found its way over the low ankle of her shoes, the tiny grains burying themselves in to the small dense loops of her terry toweling socks. They stood at the fringe of the beach lobbing stones far out and watching them plop in to the sludge.

Felicity found herself looking out to the horizon wondering when the sea would come back. Her thoughts turned; she thought about the how tides were created, the gravitational pull of the moon and sun and the spin of the earth. She suddenly felt very small, insignificant almost, and mildly dizzy.

Quiet leant down and pecked her lips. She smiled up at him.

Peanut broke the spell. 'Let's go arcades!'

As it was his idea, he chose the brightest, loudest establishment on the front. A huge yellow façade adorned with hundreds of red bulbs lured passers-by in to its inner sanctum. A swirling kaleidoscope of colours and chaotic symphony of noise numbed the senses. They played the bandits and waterfall machines, sliding spare coppers in to the slots until they were all spent out then thieving from their neighbour's pot in a desperate bid to keep the own fun going.

When all had spent their last penny, the disappointment was just too much to bear for some. As they moved on, Jan deliberately flicked her denim hip in to a waterfall machine causing a cascade of coppers to fall in to the collection tray below. The machine lights flashed manically and the alarm siren whooped splitting the already noisy air of the arcade. Alerted, the security headed towards the crime scene. With no time to collect their ill-gotten spoils the group fled the premises.

After a pit stop for a bag of salt and vinegar-soaked chips that numbed the tongue they headed for the pier. The group stopped plenty on route as they bumped in to acquaintances and caught up on plans and happenings. The general consensus was that the police were keeping a low profile with minor hassles for drunk and disorderliness. There was some disappointment that the army of mods that were rumoured to be heading for Southend to do battle with the skinheads had not turned up. Rivalry between mods and skinheads was fierce in some areas despite their shared histories and roots.

At the pier Felicity and Quiet slid away from the group for a while. They walked the length of the wooden structure as far as pedestrians were allowed. At the farthest point, they stood for a while looking way out. Felicity breathed in the view, the sea air invigorated her. She looked out as far as possible, out to the faraway where the world was once reputedly said to have ended. The outline of tanker ships broke the horizon. Though so far away they were just tiny she knew that in reality they were behemoths of the ocean. Great carriers of cargo filled with containers. It was then that Felicity spotted the movement below, the incoming of the tide. Excitedly she drew Quiet's attention to it. He joined her surprise. 'It'll come in really quick, you watch.' He pulled her to him and kissed her.

'Come on lovebirds!' Jan called to them. 'Train's going back.'

Southend pier was famous for its mini train service, a bit of fun and a blessing for those that preferred not to walk the mile and a bit of its length. The gang piled aboard and choo-chooed all the way back to terra-firma.

******

Quiet was right. By the time they had landed back on the promenade the sea was well on the push. They met a couple of North London skinheads who were happy to tell Quiet that they had stumbled across a pub that was serving skinheads despite the general lockdown. It was a small establishment, very old school; 'Run by an old original skinhead' by all accounts. They led the way to a pub well behind the sea front close to a railway line. An establishment clad in dark wood and stained glass that had the air of an establishment long left behind. Today it was threatening to burst its windows, it was packed to the rafters with skinheads.

Quiet elbowed his way to the bar. A man the size of a mature oak tree with a nose that suggested he knew his way around a boxing ring was clearly in control. The landlord was unfazed by the clientele and made sure they knew who was boss. His bar staff were flat out, their brows moist with perspiration as they pulled on pumps and pushed on optics. Getting served was a lottery, punters waving a note of whatever denomination over the bar to get the staff's attention. Those without paper money juggled coins in their palm and hoped that would be enough.

Vintage reggae and ska music was playing over the pub's speakers. Shoulders dipped and heads nodded to the rhythms. Budding Max Romeos held their women close and let their hips grind together. Being close was not an option in the confines of the pub, it was a given.

Every night mi go to sleep mi have wet dreams
Every night mi go to sleep mi have wet dreams
Lie down gal let me push it up push it up lie down
Lie down gal let me push it up push it up lie down

Quiet had a knack. He had soon caught the barmaid's eye. The woman cupped her ear straining to hear his order.

'Oi! I was waiting before you!' It was a voice he was familiar with. Quiet turned to see his old friend Jack hemmed in against the bar, his elbows swimming in pools of spilt beer. He grinned at Quiet.

'Serve him first.' Quiet advised the barmaid. He was keen to avoid any conflict.

'I'll serve who I want. Don't need big mouths like him to tell me my job.' She ignored Jack.

'Who you fuckin' calling big mouth!' Colour flared in Jack's cheeks.

'It's cool. I can wait.' Quiet reasoned with her. He turned back to Jack. 'Relax, Jack. She's just trying to do her job.'

'Then she should know who's next in line shouldn't she!'

'Listen mate, I don't like your manner.' Jack had the woman's full attention now. As she prepared to do verbal battle with Jack, the Oak of Essex moved across the bar. He had been monitoring the whole incident and decided that he needed to offer his pound of timber to the debate. 'What's the problem?' The landlord had to stoop for fear of his head clattering in to the glasses that hung from the shelving above the bar.

Jack started, 'I was next, been waiting ages!'

'I wasn't asking you.' The landlords look told Jack all that he needed to know. That he had kicked a wasp's nest and now had a choice, whether to wave his hands around and run the risk of getting stung or to remain still and wait for the danger to pass.

'He may have been next, to be fair, Harry, but I don't like the way he's speaking to me'. She explained. Harry nodded and touched her shoulder. 'Good girl, carry on with what you were doing.'

Harry positioned himself over Jack. Calmly, he reached for a bar towel. 'Friendly bit of advice, son.' He reached over and lifted Jack's elbow as he wiped the puddle of booze from beneath. 'Mind your manners in my pub.' He flipped the towel over his enormous shoulder. 'Now, what would you like to drink?'

Quiet found the others. They had set up camp near a window. It was a tight squeeze but no one seemed to mind. The atmosphere was what mattered. The music fitted the mood and those that could, danced where they stood. Quiet stood with his back to the window. His height was an asset in situations like this. He could see over most heads. He spotted Jack's sidekick Skinny across the room. Skinny stared back at him. He sneered then raised his long bony middle digit in Quiet's direction, the universal sign language for 'fuck you'. Quiet stared back at the skinny skinhead. He had nothing to prove but it was a matter of pride. He was not sure why Skinny had taken such a dislike to him, their paths had rarely crossed, but he was not going to let the man bully him. All he could think of is that his past friendship with Jack was a problem for the man. If it came to blows Quiet was confident that he would be able to handle it. The crowd in the pub ensured that a dust up between them was an unlikely scenario for the time being but Quiet knew it was only a matter of time.

Felicity nudged him from his thoughts. 'Just going for a wee.' She kissed him quickly on the lips before setting off on a mission to find the ladies toilets with Jan. By the time he looked back Skinny was out of sight. He relaxed again.

Boom! Splintering glass showered his neck and shoulders. He lurched forward with the sudden impact but somehow retained hold of his pint of lager, the liquid now laced with shards of red and green stained glass. A skinhead close to him clutched his forehead where the chunk of paving slab had hit him. Blood ran between his fingers, in rivulets down his face.

Quiet switched on. He turned to the gaping hole left in the pub window. The street outside was swarming with teddy boys, rockers and local hard men throwing bottles and bricks toward the pub. Tooled up and ready for violence they taunted the skinheads, inviting them outside to do battle. Enraged and picking glass from his collar, Quiet fought his way outside. He arrived, one of the first to toe the line. A bottle shattered around his boots.

They were faced with men. Men built for manual labour and hard drinking. Men from a bygone era, an era that they sorely missed and tried desperately to cling on to. Men that were offended by the new breed of youth that invaded their town. Men that resented the changes that these outsiders represented.

They met in the middle, a tangle of swinging arms and legs and butting heads. Quiet felt the jar of impact vibrate through his arm as his balled fist crunched in to a quiffed cranium. He let his boots fly at the rocker's kneecaps. The man slumped, Quiet drove his toecap into the side of the man's head. A motorbike chain flew and whipped, slapping itself around Quiet's head, slicing in to his cheek bones. His head was wrenched backwards, the chain tightening, biting in to flesh and finding bone. Quiet fought to free himself from the snare as his greasy haired assailant put a well-aimed biker boot in to his guts. He was winded. To his relief he felt the chain slacken. He pulled it from his face and sucked in a bellyful of air. When he looked up, Raven was bringing a stool leg down with skull splitting force on top of the greaser's head.

The tide was turning in the skinhead's favour. The teddy boys and their cohorts had not envisaged the sheer weight of numbers and willingness to fight that the skinheads would offer. They had miscalculated. The boot was going in all over the road. No quarter was given and no mercy allowed.

Satisfied that the rocker offered no further opposition due to his unconscious state, Raven focused on getting Quiet moving. He hauled unceremoniously at his skinhead comrade's shirt collar. The sound of police sirens was too close for comfort. They needed to get away from the area.

******

Felicity wriggled herself back in to her fishnet stockings before unfurling her denim mini-skirt down from around her midriff. She flushed and turned to leave the cubicle. Opening the graffiti-spattered door, she was astonished to find the previously-busy amenities now completely empty save for a couple of abandoned taps running in to sinks. She turned them off and tuned in to a rumble of noise coming through the door in to the toilet.

She opened the door in to a world of riot. Bodies pushed and shoved towards the pub's exits. She fought to get her bearings, desperately searching among the cropped heads for a sign of Quiet or Jan or anyone from the crew. It was hopeless. The first spike of panic formed in her gut, she recognised the feeling and took a deep breath through her nostrils. Her fists balled, she began to fight her way through the crowd, her sharp knees and elbows finding opportunistic gaps and prising open a narrow, claustrophobic route towards the main doors. As she neared her exit, she could hear the violence. The crowd's movements urgent, sharper. Thrown from side to side, her ears ringing with obscenities and war cries, she was eventually flung out on to the pavement where she landed on her side in a ragdoll heap.

She gathered herself immediately, hauling herself up among the flailing bodies that surrounded her, a gaping hole in her black tights framing a gashed kneecap. She paid it no mind as she tried to get to her friends, scanning the crowd for their faces. Where had they all gone?

She stepped over a leather-jacketed casualty. His studded armour had been no match for the hard soled shoes and boots of the skinheads. His face was a mess of lacerations, lumps and bruising, his eyes now only slits in puffy flesh. A skinhead girl gave him an extra kick as she passed, though his lifeless body offered no response. The area began clearing fast as police vehicles arrived on the scene, flashing lights and sirens breaking through the baying chants of the mob.

'Skinheads! Skinheads!'

She could see no one she knew. It was unnerving and she felt exposed. It was an old and familiar feeling to her but she had not felt it for some time. Her assimilation in to the established group had not taken long at all and she had soon found herself very comfortable, even safe among them. Without realizing it her previously constant need to remain alert and suspicious, both necessary traits required for survival in her earlier misadventures, had eased off and she had allowed herself to enjoy the freedoms that this new approach had awarded. The unquestioning nature of this newfound human contact had been an elixir, the group's adventures and the laughter that often accompanied them offering her a whole new life experience to that which had gone before.

And that was all fine and dandy but at this moment she required those old, inherent survival instincts if she was to find a way out of the chaos in front of her. She grabbed the skinhead girl's arm. The girl whirled on her; jet-black feathers flicked back from her eyes. She glared at Felicity's interruption.

'Which way's the front?'

"What?" The girl blew remaining strands of wispy black hair from her face, her bosom jutted out high and firm in the red, white and blue of a union jack t-shirt.

'The seafront!' Felicity made herself clearer. 'Which way is it?' She had an idea that the group would regroup somewhere along the front.

'Follow the crowd.' The girl nodded towards the exodus moving away from the pub while the coppers desperately fought to regain control of them. In reality it was too late to do anything but mop up the wounded and some drunk, disorderly remnants. The thin blue line was easily outnumbered and the skinheads, fueled up on booze and adrenaline, were not going to be stopped by such a stretched show of force.

She followed the girl in to the crowd, fighting internally with that old, careful, suspicious voice that told her to separate, to find her own way.

Like a tiny, ragtag army of youthful exuberance they advanced on the front. Day trippers stepped aside, in to the safety of doorways and off of pavements in to the road, preferring the risk of being mown down by Essex boy racers than having to weave themselves through the tightly-packed ranks of skinheads.

At the seafront she detached from the larger group and began her hunt for her friends. She was confident that they would not abandon her, that they would be doing the same in reverse; looking for her. It was something unspoken. An affection that was felt. A clear loyalty and protection that when you signed up to being part of something, came as part of the package.

She wandered along stopping occasionally to scan the promenade for familiar faces. It was a task that had become all the more challenging. The gathering of skinheads on the seafront had at least doubled. Felicity guessed that hundreds if not in to the thousands had now invaded the town. The youths were everywhere as far as she could see. Clearly disgruntled pedestrians did their utmost to give them a wide berth, scowling and dragging their children quickly away.

It was as she passed a narrow alleyway between two shops that she was knocked sideways, flying off her feet. The blow caught her completely unaware, she landed in a heap, unprotected and floundering among a pile of black bin bags stinking of domestic rubbish and cardboard boxes. As she fell, she had caught her eye on the corner of thick-walled box. She clutched the wounded area, her legs flailing uselessly above her head. Tears streamed down her cheek, the pain seared through her head, deep in to her skull, like scything bolts of white lightning. Momentarily blinded, she fought and twisted to right herself. Beneath her, black bags popped and shed their rotting loads, smearing her with smelly, slimy fluids that made her retch.

She turned herself on to her back, her hips higher than her shoulders, a mound of debris beneath her lower back. Wedged in deep, stinging nettles and thistles, the only vegetation that could survive in that damp and dirty alley, bit in to the bone of shoulders. The discomfort of her position was, however, overwhelmed by the excruciating throbbing from her freshly wounded eye socket. Through her good eye she strained to make sense of what had happened, the narrow strip of sky above her was a wet blur. She lifted her hand away from her bad eye and checked her palm. There was blood, enough to cause her concern. It stained the lines of her fingertips pink.

What had happened? She tried to sit up. Her position offered her little leverage. She grasped desperately at the plastic bags, her fingertips ripping through the thin black skin and finding soggy, mushy innards. Laughter, mocking her desperate efforts, filled the narrow void.

Startled, she wriggled and writhed harder, grunting with her struggles. She strained her neck muscles to locate the source of the cruel mirth. With her good eye, she found it and it was unpleasant enough to turn her stomach over. A long slit of a sneer sliced his face. His eyes were hard and oozing with malicious intent. It was a thin, narrow face between two large ears. His head was shaved, a number one crop, just a shadow of bristle that only enhanced his spiteful appearance. She recognised him immediately. Skinny.

He stood over her, savouring the spectacle of helplessness that he had managed to create. His long arms hung by his side, his bare tattooed chest bellowed in and out, stimulated and urgent. The inked figure of St George upon his stallion reared up, spearing the dragon with each intake of breath the man took.

'Hello sweetheart!' He hissed. 'What you doing out and about on your lonesome?' It was a rhetorical question. No answer required. He did not care.

She gave a heave in an attempt to free herself.

He laughed at her efforts. 'Where's golden boy? Do you think he will come to save your bacon?'

Felicity felt the old familiar surge of dread flood her body. It was clear that Skinny intended to do her more harm. The nature of his plans for further harm became clearer as he reached for the waistband of his jeans and popped the button of his fly, lowering his zipper.

Felicity gritted her teeth and fired a kick upwards, her oxblood shoe, pointed with ram-rod straight venom towards the man's bollocks. It thudded in to his groin but lacked enough velocity to cause him harm. He stepped back abruptly, his face turning darker and more vicious. He stooped low and punched her in the face. Her teeth bust through her upper lip, she felt the pulpy flesh thicken immediately, the taste of injury, metallic, filling her mouth. She coughed as her own blood threatened to choke her.

'That's better. I prefer it rough.' He ripped her skirt up high over her hips and wrenched her tights and knickers down to her knees. She could now feel the heat of his panting, see the glisten of saliva on his lips he was that close to her. She swung her legs around making it as awkward as possible for him. He gained control of her flailing legs with his bony knees. He had her pinned. All she could do was spit.

It was not enough.

XVIII

Quiet drove the heel of his boot down hard in to the back of the man's head. It stunned him, stopped him in his tracks momentarily but had little destructive result. It was at that moment that Quiet regretted his choice to wear his Air Wair soled boots rather than his leather soled, quarter-tipped brogues to Southend that day. How he wanted to stave the man's skull in, to split his cranium in two and to watch the sticky jam of his brains ooze out on to the floor. But the stamp had left Quiet unstable, slipping and stumbling as he tried to regain his footing among the accumulation of debris that had been dumped in the alley. By the time he had regained some balance, Skinny had twisted to face him. With his trousers down, Skinny found himself at Quiet's mercy. He acted fast, reaching to the ankle of his boot, he pulled a kitchen knife. In a moment, he thrust the weapon in a short arc, slicing through the man's army greens and sinking the steel deep in to his thigh.

Quiet's hands shot to the wound, his face turned white with shock, a dark stain spread, quickly saturating the whole of his upper thigh. Skinny was back on his feet, hitching his jeans up one handed while waving the blade threateningly in Quiet's direction.

'You fuckin' pathetic prick!' Skinny seemed to enjoy narrating his violent displays. 'Big fuckin' hero, come to save your bitch!'

Quiet had stumbled and was propped against the alley wall. His eyes wide, his skin pale as he pressed his hands hard in to his thigh trying to slow the bleed.

Skinny juggled the knife between his fingers as he secured his fly, his eyes fixed on Quiet. He sneered. 'Look at you! Not such a big man now, are you?' Skinny's tendency for overly flamboyant narrative was his weakness. Felicity swung with ferocity. She rammed the broken ketchup bottle against the side of Skinny's head. Skinny howled clutching in agony at his torn ear, a dangling mash of cartilage, flesh, blood and tomato sauce. He spun in desperate defence and clubbed at her damaged eye socket, shooting a bolt of indescribable hurt through every bone in her body. Her legs collapsed beneath her. She tried to scream, anything to alert passersby, but all that she could muster was a strangled squeak.

Skinny flicked the loose pieces of flesh from his fingers and glared at her.

Any earlier notions he had of raping Felicity had dissipated. Quiet's intervention, as irritating as it was, had only changed the game. His focus now was on payback. The girl had mutilated him, he could tell that his ear was virtually severed and the bitch was going to pay. He moved forward with intent and anticipation as he weighed the knife in his palm.

******

The knife shot from his hand as a force thudded in to his lower back. The blood-soaked steel disappeared among the rubbish. Skinny twisted his torso like a hooked eel engaging in a frantic wrestling match to gain the upper hand over his attacker. They were quickly locked in contact, arms grappling as both men fought for space to make an attack. Skinny withstood the thud of short blows against his head as he brought his knees up and thrust them in to the torso of his attacker, sending the assailant up and away from him. He froze, gawping up at the figure stood over him.

'Jack? What the fuck?'

Jack answered. He stamped his brogue heel down hard on to Skinny's astonished face easily breaking his nose. He followed up, turning Skinny's features in to a bloody map of lacerated flesh and broken bone in a matter of seconds.

Jack reached in among the jumble of bags and boxes and pulled Felicity clear. She shrugged him off. 'I'm fine. Help Jim!' She barked. Her Jim, Quiet, was slumped on his backside against the wall oblivious to the follow up violence that had erupted less than a couple of feet away from him. He had clearly lost a significant amount of blood. Jack knelt by him and pressed his hands in to his thigh. 'Get help!'

Felicity was already on her way, stumbling and tripping towards the main road.

Chaos reigned in the street beyond the alley. It was no wonder her cries for help had gone unnoticed. Bodies ran from one end of the promenade to the other, this way and that. Police officers grabbed at skinhead youths, wrestling them to the floor then throwing them in to the backs of waiting meat wagons with all the dignity of refuse bags being flung in to the back of a dust cart. She searched frantically for someone who could help.

Hard hands grabbed her arms. She looked down at the dark blue material of a police tunic.

'Stop!' she pleaded. 'You need to help me. My boyfriend has been hurt. Please, listen to me.'

The officers ignored her pleas, intent on getting their catch to the nearest meat wagon. She deliberately dragged her feet, creating a dead weight for the two officers as they pulled her further away from the injured Quiet and any chance of getting him the help he needed. She lifted her head to see a waiting police van.

'Please! I'm serious. Where are you taking me? I've done nothing wrong!' She twisted hard but was unable to break their grasp. Her earlier battles had left her in a weakened state. Her eye was closed shut, her swollen mouth made speaking difficult, every bone, hair and cell on her body hurt.

'Maybe you should have stayed at home like a good girl.' The coppers lack of sympathy was clear. His weekend leave had been abruptly cancelled when the skinhead train had arrived in sunny Southend. He had a bone to pick with the numbskulls who had decided to spoil his plans for a round of golf and a few bevvies in the clubhouse.

As they approached the rear of the van, Felicity realized that it would be her last chance to break free, to get Quiet the assistance he so desperately needed. She kicked out wildly at the copper's shins. Her assault was enough to send them both stumbling downwards on to the hard road surface. Unprotected knee bones crunched in to the unforgiving tarmac. 'You little cow!' He had her pinned to the floor, the well-placed forearm of the long arm of the law wedged hard against her cheek, aggravating her eye injury. He was heavy, she had no chance of shifting him, another copper arrived to help. Grabbing her kicking legs, he tugged roughly at the heel of her shoes, pulling them from her feet. 'You won't be needing these again will you, Kevin Keegan!'

Felicity could only watch in horror, the loss etched across her face, as her coveted oxblood shoes were tossed away in to the gutter. All fight in her was depleted. She slumped under the weight of the restraint. They lifted her up easily. Her bloody bare knees were peppered with grit, her tights were shredded like an old spider web, gaped and torn. Snot, blood and tears marbled her face, her once pretty features, now puffy and bruised like an old potato.

The doors of the van were opened and ready. Sitting close to the door, the outstretched arm of the female copper held the door handle ready to slam it shut once Felicity was deposited. Much of the other bench seating was already occupied by other youths, all skinheads, who had been unlucky enough to be rounded before her. The woman officer grasped her arm and pulled her in to the rear of the van. 'Get in, sit down, shut up.'

Felicity did as she was told. She was too exhausted to argue. She flopped down on to the hard seating opposite the officer. Her head almost dropped to the floor between her knees. When she looked up, she noticed the woman assessing her. Her injuries were significant, despite her tough bitch act the officer was clearly concerned.

'My boyfriend,' Felicity croaked. Her throat was dry and raw, her lips stuck together with clotted blood and mucus. 'He's been hurt. Really hurt bad.'

'He'll be picked up, love.' The woman was trying to remain detached but the tag of 'love' at the close of her response was a clear sign that she felt some empathy.

'He's been stabbed.' Felicity swallowed hard, trying to free up her vocal cords. 'In the leg. He's bleeding bad.' The WPC turned her head away, looking out through the barred rear window in to a street of chaos.

The closed rear door offered some detachment from the scene outside, the rear glass, dusty and screened in protective mesh., was like a porthole to another world, bizarre, almost comedic. Figures beyond it moved quickly to and fro, a silent film mixed with slapstick and ultra-violence.

A hefty thud rocked the van. The rear window now shadowed by writhing bodies caught in a death struggle. It jolted Felicity from her near catatonic state. The WPC sprung to action, unlocked the door and flung it wide open. Sandwiched between two sweating coppers was Jack.

They could barely contain him as he wrestled, twisting and thrusting to break their grip. Their silver-nippled helmets were hanging on by a prayer and a chin strap. Clenched fists welding truncheons had been rendered ineffective as the officers concentrated their efforts on restraining on him.

Jack's face was one of fury, his skin flushed brutal red, white-hot spittle flying from his mouth as he yelled the foulest of obscenities. His striped button-down shirt was torn wide open at the placket, all of its buttons lost, the oxford cloth material billowing out like storm-torn sails. He wedged a boot against the rear step to stop them pushing him in to the van, the officers heaved but could not shift him. The WPC reacted instantly to support her colleagues, she tried to wrestle Jack's boot away from the step.

At that moment, their eyes met momentarily; Felicity's one good one and Jacks wildly-dilated pair. She could swear she saw him wink at her.

Felicity shoved the woman hard on her buttocks. Her balance already compromised the WPC was unable to prevent momentum taking her. She toppled heavily out of the van landing awkwardly in to the tangle. Felicity reacted instantly, wasting no time or opportunity, she was out and over the pile of bodies in an instant. Despite her condition, adrenalin took over, she held the advantage, she was balanced, on her feet and agile.

She grimaced as the spongy flesh of her feet hit the road, her terry-toweling socks no match for the rough, gritty surface. There was no time to retrieve her treasured Dr Marten shoes. She spun urgently. Her bearings were lost. Activity was everywhere, it was all so disorientating. She searched frantically for the alleyway. Her eyes scanned, full circle, yet she could not locate it.

With realization, she looked again and saw the ambulance, its rear doors wide open, blocking the alleyway. Around it, emergency services and police-men bustling with urgency. She allowed herself a few moments to take in the scene, staying alert and ready to move if needed. She took a sharp intake of breath as a trolley rattled noisily to the rear of the ambulance. She breathed out with some small relief as she saw that it was Quiet. His head propped up on a pillow. He looked conscious, just.

She fought the urge to run over to the ambulance. Her heart twisting, tearing inside, almost overwhelming her logic. The scene was swarming with activity, emergency services were all over it, enough police presence to keep the perime-ter locked down. Her disheveled state would certainly raise scrutiny and un-wanted questions. She had only just escaped from the van. She could not afford to be taken in.

Not then, not ever.

Her heart was mincemeat but her head was in gear. Satisfied that Quiet was in safe hands, she turned and began to run.

She wove through the remnants of the disturbance, her stride punctuated with stumbles caused by weakness and injury. Her feet were soon on fire. Every foot strike flaying more skin from her soles. Every small piece of grit burrowing in to her flesh.

But she kept running. Quick and steady, along the seafront. If the pavement was crowded, she dropped down off the curb in to the road but she could allow nothing to stop her momentum. She needed distance.

She recognised familiar places from earlier in the day, ignoring their stares as she flew past the Kursal and kept going, straight, following the road that ran alongside the beach but away from the devastation behind her. She sucked in the pungent sea air, the crucial fuel filling the demand from her lungs, and forced her limbs in to a rhythm. She kept the motor running until she was sat-isfied that she was far enough away from it all.

She slowed and slowed until she was barely hobbling. Her knees almost col-lapsing. She stepped over a low wall on to the beach. There, she dropped down on to her bum and leant back against the hard seawall, her small chest heaving with exertion. As her breathing settled, she drew her legs up wrapping her forearms around her shins. She blinked as if waking from a terrible dream. White light sparkled off the water making her squint. Sand blew up in little whirlwinds dusting her wounds. Her face was significantly damaged, her eye swollen shut, its socket most likely fractured, if not broken. Her lip was fat and torn.

Seagulls squawked along the flat shore, brash and loud. Fighting over left-behind chips and pastry. She stared out at the ripples on the water. On the horizon the big ships she had watched earlier in the day were still there, moving freight, backwards and forwards through the Thames Estuary. Obviously, not the same ships as earlier but proof if needed that despite all that had gone on, some things just kept moving.

It all seemed so detached. Even those events most recent, the commotion she had fled were almost certainly still in motion. The images in her head appeared vague and indistinct, like a forgotten length of negative film that had been left in the bottom of a drawer somewhere. She made no effort to gain focus, to recollect. It did not matter now. Sitting on the beach, her buttocks nestled in to the soft sand, she knew that all that had occurred since running from the home was history.

She knew that she should be feeling a certain way. Quiet had been hurt badly. She had been hurt too, almost raped and maimed. And yet, she felt a calmness around her. An acceptance of things the way they were. She guessed she should have been in pieces, a snotty, sniveling, sobbing mess.

But she was not.

She had no urgency to move. She was comfortable. There was no rush now. She would rest a while. She reached out and plucked a small empty shell from the sand rubbing her thumb across the ripples. She breathed in long and deep. She imagined that she could feel the energy of the sea flooding in to her lungs and nourishing her beaten state.

She stood and pulled her top up and over her head, dropping it to the sand. She wriggled her short skirt off her hips, past her thighs, over the remnants of her black tights and stepped out of the ruck of denim. She pulled the remnants of her socks off her raw feet. She walked to edge where the sea met the sand. She glanced at a small child filling a colourful bucket with seawater for his moat he had made. The scene made her smile, stretching her wounded lip. The sea lapped at her toes. Inviting her. She stepped in and began wading, headed for the horizon. The yawning vastness of the Thames estuary beckoned, drawing her in. The cool sea water soaked in to her wounds, cooling, healing.

She continued on, past the tiny ripples of wave action. Feeling the squidge of the Essex mud between her toes. In past her knees, past her waist, up over her belly button. The cold penetrated deep, numbing her flesh, burrowing to her bones.

She felt no need to check back at the shoreline. She knew that she had been wading for a while. Satisfied, she stopped, took a deep breath and dropped beneath the surface.

Her instinct would tell her what to do next.

IXX

Felicity fiddled with the last small piece between her fingers. Gazing out of the window, her position awarded a great view across the grounds and over the Essex countryside. It was a settled early summer morning as she sat, a thousand-piece jigsaw almost complete spread across a large table top.

She brought her attention back to the puzzle. The image when completed would show a map of London. Specifically, those areas that spread out along the banks of the river Thames. The waterway meandered through the centre of the image, interrupted along its length by bends and eleven bridges. The riverside was dotted with famous landmarks of London; The Houses of parliament, Cleopatras needle, The Globe theatre, HMS Belfast, Tower of London, The Docklands, Greenwich. It was a colourful and busy scene.

As she had completed the task over a few weeks she had allowed herself to imagine what these places were like in her head. She had tried to see herself walking the embankment, looking across the great tidal serpent whose belly rippled with currents. She imagined herself stopping along the way to watch as the river flow was disrupted by obstructions, the water disturbed and broiling, as it fought to get around the abutments built to support the busy bridges that spanned its breadth. She had wondered what it would be like to step on to the famous Tower Bridge, following its gentle curve over the river and to look up at the huge ancient towers that made it such an awe-inspiring sight. She wondered how long it took to cross from one side to the other.

The piece of the jigsaw she fiddled with held significance. That tiny piece of printed cardboard, at that moment, symbolized an end; closure. Her sixteenth birthday had marked change for her.

It did not come as a surprise. She had known for a long time that her residence at the home was coming to an end. The home catered for children and, although she was not quite an adult, she had outgrown the place, at least, in the eyes of the board who ran it. They had made plans for her. She had not had a lot of say in any decisions made but she was resigned to it. She had not had much of a say in what happened to her for a very long time.

A child arrived at the table. 'Mister Benfield said can you come to the office?' At the boy's words, she felt a chill to the marrow of her bones. Any peace she had felt was shattered, the bottle of anxiety she held within burst, spearing shards of glass in to her gut. She thanked the boy and he toddled off.

She focused on the giant puzzle before her, leaning across she carefully laid the final piece in to the remaining space.

Completed, she rose off the seat and with a deliberate sweep of her arm, sent all thousand pieces scattering across the floor.

******

His door was open, waiting for her. She stepped in to the office that had always stank of cigarette smoke and stale coffee. The man sat at his desk, behind filing trays, an old tea mug full of pens, piles of cardboard files held together with little cord ties, a dark green telephone and an ashtray cradling a cigarette. Smoke spiraled wastefully up towards the ceiling joining the smog that was already there. 'Oh Felicity! Thank you for coming so quickly.' Mister Benfield welcomed her with a long smile. 'Take a seat.'

She remained standing and silent.

Recognising that she was not going to close the door behind her, he lifted himself out of the chair using both hands on the rests, skimmed around her and closed it himself. He moved back behind his desk. 'So, Felicity. How are things with you?'

Again, she remained silent. She had little to say.

'Ok.' He brought his hands together, linking his fingers. 'Well, it seems our time together is short. You have grown in to a handsome young woman and I am sure you will go on to do very well whatever direction you choose to take from here. I hope that you will be happy with the arrangements that have been made for your further care?' He pulled a file towards himself. He opened it scanning the documents within. 'Nine years old when you came to us.' He shook his head lightly. 'Seems like yesterday, does it not?' He looked up in expectation. Felicity held his eye contact.

She hated the man's dense, greasy hair combed tightly back towards the back of his neck; it stank of cheap hair oil. She despised his scratchy moustache, tarred at the tips by his twenty-a-day habit. Her stomach turned at the sight of his discoloured teeth; no amount of scrubbing with smoker's paste could remove the stain of coffee and fags from the enamel or cure his gingivitis. She felt sick at the sight of his intertwined fingers, the stain of nicotine yellowing the tips.

She felt it all.

'You know,' He began, almost conspiratorially, 'Our paths became entwined for a reason. I had not long held this office. It was very new to me. Your arrival here soon after was almost destined. I don't know if you believe in that sort of thing?' He took his cigarette from the ashtray and took a long hard drag. He dotted the remainder out and sat back in his chair before letting out a stream of thick, silver smoke. 'I knew you were special the moment I saw you. That's why I chose you.' He nodded towards her. 'And history tells me that I was right to do so.'

Felicity felt the walls of the office closing in around her. Her vision had become tunneled. All other parts of the office were obliterated, her peripheral vision gone. All her focus was on Mister Benfield.

'I called you in to discuss our arrangement.' He looked down at the file then raised his head. 'What we had between us was special, I believe I have made that clear. Our meetings meant everything to me and I shall miss them dearly.' He continued. 'Tonight, as is usual I would you to come here, soon after lights out. Same time as always.' He checked to see that he held her attention before adding. 'With a small change.'

Felicity felt the old, cold, spike of fear.

'Yes, tonight I would like you to bring your friend. The young lady that you seem to enjoy spending much of your time with. Bring her along with you.' He made it sound convivial. 'Georgina, isn't it?'

Felicity broke her silence. 'She's ten years old! She'll be asleep!'

He looked up sternly. 'I am well aware of that! Your support will ensure that she feels comfortable. I would like you to ensure that she settles quickly. Late privileges are for special girls, you know that, that is why you're here.' He turned back to the files on his desk. He did not look up. "Please do not be late.'

Felicity stood paralyzed, sick to her marrow. She felt unable to command her limbs to cooperate, rooted to the spot.

Mister Benfield, perturbed, looked up from his desk and helped her along her way. 'Still here? You can leave now.' As he saw it, they could just as easily have been chatting about the weather.

******

Felicity ate little at tea that evening. She sat with Georgina as was usual and encouraged her to eat her vegetables. Teatimes were noisy at the home. Many of the children were very young and had high energy. Felicity liked this. It added a vibrancy to the place. At the close of tea, the children were allowed some time to play and to watch tv before bedtime routines began. Felicity chose to spend time with Georgina. She enjoyed playing with Lego bricks, building houses and making up little scenarios. Felicity loved to see her happy.

And yet, it was with a heavy heart that she spent those precious moments with her young friend. She knew that their time together was coming to an end very soon.

She thought back to her own arrival at the home. Confused, frightened and lost she had been lucky enough to have been looked after by Mary, one of the carers. Mary had settled her in and made her feel safe and comfortable. She had enjoyed those early days. She got on well with most and it was fun to have so many other children to play with. Things had been okay for her for a while.

That was all before Mister Benfield had marked her.

While she knelt with Georgina, she tried not to look up at the big wall clock too often.

******

At the little one's bedtime, she hugged the little girl for quite some time, pulling her tight until she squeaked that she was suffocating. When she let go, Georgina went off to her bedtime chores. The girl had no idea that would be the last time she would see Felicity.

Felicity was the last to leave the lounge. It was much later, her seniority among the girls gave her extra privileges. She got up and scanned the room. The care staff were happily engaged and did not award her a second glance. Nothing was unusual. In another hour or two, there would be a change-over in staff as the night duty officers took over. She needed things to look normal. As is usual she went to her room and fetched her toiletries. She did everything that she would normally do. She bathed and said her good nights before heading to her room. It was getting late. The halls were quiet and the lighting had been lowered. Once there she allowed herself time to collect herself. She knew what needed to be done. She slipped a sweatshirt over her t-shirt and cord jeans. Reaching down she found the small tear she had made in the seam of her mattress, squeezing her hand in to the opening, she pulled out the contraband she had hidden there previously.

Cursing the home procedures that locked their footwear away every night, she made her way down the hall in her socks. She was stealthy ensuring that she did not bump in to any of the staff.

She arrived at Mister Benfield's office, took a deep breath and rapped on the door.

'Come in.'

It was an effort not to vomit.

His face lit up as she entered. He was stood, leaning against the desk. He had removed his suit jacket and taken off his tie allowing his shirt collars to billow out. His presence this late at the office was never questioned. No one would dare. Anyway, most staff just assumed he was still working.

As he always did, he squeezed by her and threw the big key, locking them both in. She purposely allowed her mind to race, energizing her and spiking her adrenalin. The traumatic familiarity of the room wrenched at her emotions but she knew that she needed to maintain control. In her head, she replayed the man's whispered encouragements. The manicured compliments. The carefully designed warnings he would administer that would prevent her speaking out.

Years of his sordid expectations and demands inflamed her stomach. Her skin crawled as she recalled the unapologetic touching; uninvited and unrequited.

She remembered the first time he had invaded her pre-pubescent body and the bleeding that had followed. She remembered the weekly summonses that followed.

She allowed the rage within her to boil.

It was as he turned from the door that he noticed that she had not brought Georgina to him as directed. Concern etched his face. 'Where is Georgina?' He moved towards her. Felicity remained rooted to her spot as he continued.

'I told you to bring her!' He hissed at her. He could not shout for fear of alerting other staff so he got much closer to her. So close that Felicity felt the heat of his breath smear her face.

She finally spoke, 'You'll never have Georgina.'

As he moved to grasp her shoulder, she whipped her hand free from her back pocket. The silver fork flashed as she plunged the prongs in to the man's neck. Her aim was true and the impact punctured the man's carotid artery. Her human biology lessons had been most useful. She pulled the piece of cutlery free allowing thin spurts of claret to rain over the office. Immediately, she attacked again, burying the improvised weapon in to the same area.

And again.

And again.

She stared with hate in to his eyes as they spread wide with horror. The man had no time to scream or offer any defence, within an instant she had rammed the fork in to his wind pipe, the action delivered with such force that the prongs buckled, hooking them to wrecked cartilage. Her bloody hand slipped free from the weapon leaving it there impaled, protruding from his throat like a bizarre piece of jewelry. He toppled hard, uncontrolled and face down. The impact drove the fork in further, the crunch audible as his airway was completely destroyed.

Felicity allowed herself a moment.

She watched, as the man's muscles gave their last convulsions, twitching and grasping at fast fading hope. Frothy, gelatinous blood and fluid bubbled from the throat wounds. Blood splatter decorated the floor and walls of the office.

All sound then ceased.

She was satisfied that she had done all she could.

THE END

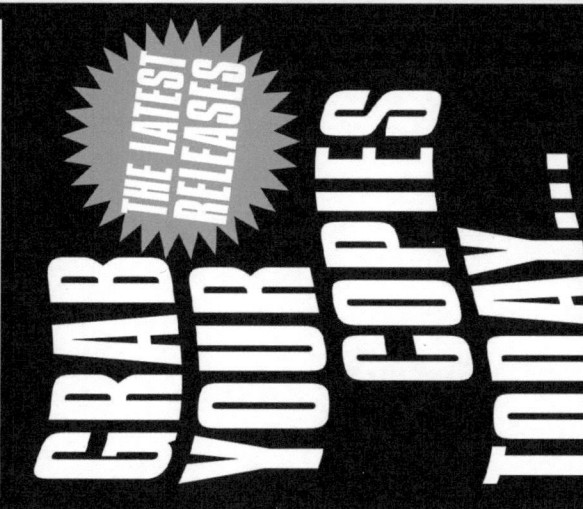

THE NEW KIDS ON THE BLOCK
www.olddogbooks.net